Renegades

Book 2 of the Wildblood

S. A. Hoag

Renegades: Book 2 of The Wildblood

Copyright © 2016, 2025 S. A. Hoag

ISBN 978-1-966538-02-8

Contents

To everyone that believed I could. So I did.

Chapter One

Estes Park morning Feb 10

"There are a dozen sets of eyes on you."

Wade stopped and turned to wait for Taylor, knowing he was there before the other man spoke. A perk, if it could be called that, of his unusual abilities. His genetically enhanced abilities. "I'm aware."

Taylor nodded, adjusting the hood of his parka as the wind came up. All the months were cold, but February was the worst. "Subtlety isn't your strong point. You want them to see you, to know you're here right now, rather than where?"

"Does it matter?" He continued walking the empty plaza, having worked up to twenty laps a morning and ten more at dusk. Considering he'd come close to dying not even a month earlier, an ambitious undertaking.

"Yes. You sent Shannon off with Vance to look at a detonation site. If it makes me wonder, you can bet I'm not the only one."

"Say what you're here to say," Wade told him. "Better yet, ask the question you're here for."

"Why?"

"Why did I send my partner and her second out to survey a radiation field that's not that far from here? That's the reason. It's not far from here. Green won't get downwind of it. Shan won't get into a situation she can't deal with."

"I'm your second, and I can tell when you're evading."

"Can you?" He had doubts.

"We came out here to take care of a Nomad problem and found another one, an entire city run by a Gen En, an Altered, that's more an enemy than ally. He's like you, but not at all like you. The idea has crossed my mind that you sent her or Green to eliminate him."

"You're right, that this raised suspicions. Vance has Cooper riding shotgun. No, we didn't plan an assassination."

"Another one, you mean." Taylor had been part of the intricate plot against Vance's former partner, Rafe. It hadn't been subtle. The team of Vistans had blown the side out of a mountain to get at him.

"If that were the case, I'd do it myself. I sure as hell wouldn't involve Shan. What we did wasn't out of a need for revenge, but to protect The Vista. You've seen what he was capable of."

"Are you so certain Vance wasn't part of what happened?"

"No, I'm not. One reason we're still here in Colorado when we have business at home."

"But we're not doing anything about the problem." Taylor might be his second, his backup officer, but he wasn't always aware of what Wade was up to. No one was.

"Without proof? We stay here and figure it out. If one of us would say 'get to the airfield five minutes ago', there's a problem that's been dealt with. Don't stop and ask questions, don't stop for anything." By 'one of us,' he meant Team Three, his team, the trio of Allen, Wade, and MacKenzie. Mac would be returning to their outpost in Cody soon. It was part of a larger plan.

"When are we going to go home, to The Vista, barring any great emergency?"

"You got to the real question."

Taylor shrugged.

"I don't know."

"That's the fall back answer all three of you use. Convenient, but a lie most of the time."

"We'll go back when Command makes it an order, when the weather changes, or when there's no other choice."

The answer didn't make Taylor feel any better.

The blast radius wasn't obvious at first. As the single-engine aircraft gained altitude, the destruction became more evident. Nothing had grown in the valley for decades, and even a layer of snow didn't hide the scar.

"An air burst," Vance said, directing the video monitor east. He spoke as the plane banked around, recording in case they wanted to view it later. "It happened early in the morning, before nine, on a Tuesday. The other detonation is south, over downtown Denver, and we suspect a third at the airport, all within minutes." He recited it like reading from a textbook. One of his guests wasn't old enough to remember. The other hadn't been born.

"Rocky Flats," Shannon said, concentrating. The facility had manufactured nuclear weapons for decades. An array of buildings were unrecognizable but for the photos they'd shown her with a brief history lesson. Anything that remained was a stark reminder of what happened that day in August.

She felt no ghosts, no impressions of the past crowding into her thoughts. This place, empty... null. The war was twenty years past. The voices faded.

What remained of civilization was scattered enclaves hidden away and guarding against other remnants of humanity. Her home, The Vista, one of those places. Vance's city, Estes Park, another. Their alliance, created to stop a common enemy, balanced on the precarious.

"Anything?" Green asked. Today he was piloting, and there to do what she told him.

She wrinkled her nose, distracted. "No, nothing that needs to be mentioned." Flying was her aversion, one she hadn't been able to avoid.

"What does that mean?" Cooper asked, the first thing he'd said during their journey. He'd taken the seat behind Vance and kept to himself. That was his job, to make sure Vance stayed safe and out of trouble. The Vistans numbered only a few, but a dangerous few. Trouble.

"It means she sees what we see," Green offered. Not Gen En but Siksika, a Blackfoot, and another misplaced Vista Security officer. Being her bodyguard for a couple of hours was a duty he requested. She was adept at controlling tricky situations, and they had each other's trust. Their relationship was far more complicated than most people believed.

Vance nodded. He'd been in charge of Estes Park for over a decade. The areas south proved troublesome, even for him. Most of central Colorado now fell under his protection, but there was a large and empty landscape where Denver once stood. Even the scavengers kept clear.

The Vista lay far to the north, past his influence. When they arrived on his doorstep months earlier, it hadn't been a complete surprise. They'd been hunting a former colleague. Rafe had tested their defenses, the outcome unexpected. Young, brash, and looking to retaliate, the Vistans accomplished in weeks what he hadn't been able to. Rafe was gone, leaving Vance in control of The Front Range.

The camera continued to rotate east, then south. "Got it," Green said, watching the feed. Their radiation scanners hadn't moved, his primary concern. Instability in the atmosphere, ranging from normal readings to dangerous ones, in the space of a few miles. By air, those miles could go by almost unnoticed.

"The weather isn't so bad today," Vance told Shannon, aware of her discomfort. It didn't take enhanced senses to see that. He tested their resolve when the opportunity happened. His latent abilities, a far cry from theirs. She'd proven that, along with Wade, during their time in Estes Park.

Green landed the plane on a long, straight section of highway. The Cessna slowed, wheels crunching in the gravel as he parked it where it stopped. No traffic, and there wouldn't be any time in the foreseeable future, save for the occasional recon plane Vance sent out. Like today.

After a quick look around, Green offered Shannon a hand down. Vance let himself out of the passenger's side, followed by Cooper. They all knew why he was there. What amounted to being the governor of Colorado, Vance made enemies over the years to achieve the distinction.

Not long ago, Cooper had threatened to shoot Shannon, on Vance's order. Green hadn't forgotten and knew she hadn't either.

Shan didn't need help to get out of the tiny airplane. She didn't need his protection, but accepted it. Safety in numbers.

The ruins across the valley were obvious, and downwind. Spring storms could kick up clouds of radioactive dust with little warning. "If this," Green tapped the patch, a radiation monitor he'd placed on the front of her parka, "beeps even once, we're gone."

She peered at the buildings in the distance, trying to imagine the people that might have been there, attempting to shift her unstable abilities into gear. Before the war, the world was a place she wouldn't recognize. After a few minutes, Shan sat down on the edge of the pavement, running her fingers through the dirt on the side of the road, humming an unknown tune to herself. Dark hair, green eyes, lithe, tall; men looked twice when they met her, and she was aware of the effect. Sometimes an advantage, usually a hindrance.

Standing nearby, they waited while Vance walked up and down the blacktop, never more than a few yards, stopping to check the time. Cooper watched Green, he watched Vance, and he never let Shannon out of his line-of-sight. As Green was about to tell Shan her ten minutes were up, she stood, slapping her hands together to dust them off.

"I've never crossed a place so empty," she announced. "Not so much empty as barren, void. It's like the bombs wiped away anything that ever happened here." Impossible to explain to them, she knew Wade would understand. They shared a psychic link, for as long as she could remember, an accidental effect of their engineered abilities. "Whatever secrets Rafe hid, he's going to keep."

"Do you still think he had a stockpile of nukes?" Green asked.

"I never thought he did. He said it to scare me. He said a lot of things."

"If he had them, they're lost now," Vance added his insight. "What Rafe's connection was to this place, I don't know. Left over from before things fell apart." They all nodded, not having much else to say. They were there to appease Wade.

"Time's up," Green said. They piled back into the plane. He didn't waste time getting into the air and heading north. Weather in the afternoon turned windy, which would make Shan less than pleasant. He wasn't certain if flying scared her, but it made her short on patience. "Estes Park, estimated touch down in twenty-two minutes."

"Not twenty-five? You can give a rough estimate and no one will mind," Shan told him, relieved to be on the move.

"I hadn't seen a working airplane before three summers ago. Don't mess with my routine." He remained stoic.

Vance and Cooper exchanged concerned glances. Inexperienced pilots in the mountains died fast, right along with their passengers.

"I'd like to get back in one piece," she said, nudging him with her shoulder, aware he'd said it to throw the others off-guard.

"With all due respect, Captain, you're the biggest distraction I have right now." The city wasn't secure, in his opinion, but not being a senior officer, he didn't get a say in the matter. He'd told Shan of his concerns.

"Shut up," she answered, not serious. Wade would tell them both to relax, or jump off a cliff, depending on his mood when they reported in, which depended on how much rest he'd gotten.

"Is that an order?"

"When have I ever given you an order?"

"I could say, but it's inappropriate."

"Okay then, we're back to shut up."

"Part of the team that killed Rafe," Vance marveled. He viewed them as little more than obstinate children. Sometimes, he was correct.

"I have other hobbies," Shan said to none of them in particular. "Beside annoying you, I mean."

"I understand you won't tell me anything about this venture," Vance said. "That information is at Wade's discretion."

Shan let him go on thinking that. They made decisions as a team and had from the beginning. There were too many things they'd never understand, as long as they stayed isolated in The Vista. Estes Park was part of that confinement now.

"Have we heard from the Airborne Scouts yet? Taylor could joke all he wanted—he didn't qualify for the job. Shannon was his twin, a fact few were aware of. Another, that there weren't two Vistan Gen Ens, there were three. Vance suspected, but he couldn't prove a thing. That elusive third wasn't Taylor.

"I'll tell you what to pass on to Cody as soon as I talk to them," Wade said, glad there was no line at the cafeteria. Too early. Someone came in to cook a meal once a day at their lodge, and a hot meal was better than whatever they'd make later. He wasn't hungry, but he needed the calories, the protein, and the stimulant.

"When are you deciding on our summer schedule? There are over fifty people in Cody, waiting."

"Cody belongs to Mac," Wade told him. "So it's not my concern."

"After all the planning, you're passing?" Taylor had his reasons.

He'd back Mac up any time, that's what Security did, but they weren't friends.

"I need to be here, in Colorado. This is the flash point and we need Cody to be secure, just in case. Anyone else can request to go home. We'll have at least a few flights north over the summer to rotate officers. I've already put you on the short list." Both had families they wanted to see. Wade's third child would be born in a few weeks; Taylor's first, a newborn when he'd met her, months ago. While some practiced monogamy, like Taylor, most of the younger generation did not. Wade, and all of Team Three were the latter, but Wade in particular. He liked women, all women, of no particular type. With his dark and rugged features, blue eyes, and unruly hair, he had no problem attracting them.

"Shan is a Scout and there's a good chance I'll have her doing that," Wade continued. "We have a lot of potential right now for figuring out what everyone is so afraid of." There was something more at play, something he hadn't been able to unravel yet.

"Everything we've done since September will cause a lot of trouble," Taylor said. "For you, for me, for all of us."

"Command issued the orders. We're separate from Council for good reasons. A time not so long ago, I didn't understand why."

"Now it's a little clearer." Taylor understood the conversation wouldn't diverge off from what they had planned, either. Team Three members were all in Security Command, and he suspected Command had known about the Gen En before there was a Team Three.

"We take the advantage of being out here without a dozen people shouting orders at us, and find out what we can," Wade said. He finished eating, his radio beeping as he stood.

Taylor shook his head. "Shan and Green," he figured. Their timing was uncanny.

"Let's find out." He answered the call. "Go ahead."

"On the ground," Green reported. "Cooper and Vance are going in to town now. As soon as Shan finishes barfing up her breakfast, we'll be around to meet you." A few moments of static, then, "She wants to know if you got that. Otherwise, we have video."

"I did," Wade said. "Bring it along, anyway. We can use it as a training video for incoming officers. Throw in a history lesson."

A little annoyed at himself for not knowing they'd been in contact with each other, Taylor had nothing to say. It was a new thing, communicating when they weren't asleep. Their abilities were changing, out in the world.

"Tell her it felt off. Weird," Wade said.

"That's what she said. We'll be there in a few minutes."

"Is Mac joining us? For the season, I mean." Taylor said. They'd been careful about maintaining Mac's cover. He was in charge of the expedition, and the fact he had a hand in everything didn't draw suspicions.

"He'll be here when we need him." Wade wouldn't expound on the statement. In his mind, the less Taylor–and anyone not on the team–knew, the less danger they were in. After the battle with Rafe, Wade wanted to involve as few people as possible, even if it meant sending the remaining officers home. Any way he considered it, he planned on having every Vistan out of Estes Park by snowfall. They'd lost two. He had no intention of losing any others.

Hunter had already gone south with a trade caravan to be reunited with the family he'd been separated from during the war. It diffused the growing tension between him and Wade, at least temporarily. A situation none of them wanted to be dealing with, and Hunter was doing them all a favor by going if he knew it or not. Wade was uncomfortable with him being Shan's new second.

"I won't commit mutiny on Mac."

"As if you would get away with it," Wade said. They'd had this conversation before.

"You think Council has a spy. It's not me."

Wade nodded. "You couldn't conceal something like that from Shannon." Even as he said it, he wondered.

"Or you."

"True enough." They made their way from the cafeteria back across the plaza. As usual, the hotel, their quarters, sat empty. Everyone scattered during the day, if they had an assignment or not.

It was getting cloudy in the west. Conditions were never ideal for flying and it would be worse later, when the wind came up. Flash blizzards could leave three feet of snow over a frozen landscape in a matter of hours, especially in February.

"Looks like snow," Wade announced with false enthusiasm.

"Since you can't tell me anything, is the weather the only reason we're still here?" Taylor asked. Colorado had always been cold in the winter, but harsher now. Nuclear winter had been a controversial subject, right up until it happened.

"Let's say yes," Wade told him. "Don't trust that the things you see or hear are the absolute truth. Not now, not until all three of us are in The Vista together, telling you."

"You're always planning your next move, or the one after that. The rest of us catch up when we can." Taylor eyed him for a moment. "Are you breaking up Team Three?"

"Because we won't be in the same place means nothing."

"The rest of us will be in Cody, or The Vista, waiting for what?"

"Command has trained us for this, to go see what's left of the world, or at least, the immediate Rocky Mountain region. You'll be waiting for orders to back us up if we need it, and doing the jobs you're supposed to be doing to keep Cody running and The Vista safe."

"What if it's the same out there as every other place we've looked?"

"Then we'll know. Vance has given us minimal information. Trade routes, big towns, little towns, Nomads looking to settle. Bits of civilization. Things we've always speculated about."

"They lied to keep us isolated."

"They've been through the end of their world. I understand why. I don't have to agree with them."

Mac and Quinlen circled each other in a pretend boxing match. All the Vista Security officers were trying to keep active, but being confined in a strange place left little in the way of options. Cabin fever. They had the same issue in Montana during the long, cold winters, but this wasn't home.

"If you don't pay more attention," Quinlen warned, "I'm going to give my C.O. one hell of a black eye."

"Don't be sad when you fail," Mac taunted, taking a swipe at him. "You're slow. Taylor is slow. Hell, Green can be too."

"I've watched Green beat the daylights out of you during practice."

"I didn't say I was perfect." They dodged around for a few more minutes until Mac saw Quinlen getting fatigued. He dropped his hands, calling it quits. "I'm not using you as a punching bag."

"I'd rather not be a punching bag," Quinlen agreed. It had been mere weeks since their incursion. He'd been injured and lost his partner. "Maybe later."

"Like this autumn," Mac figured.

"I plan on being out of here by then."

"When you're ready, let any of us know. We're all on standby." Evacuation orders, and he'd debriefed them on the situation. If they started getting comfortable, he'd send them for a week in Cody to wake them up.

"So," Quinlen made conversation, the rest of his day comprising physical therapy at the main hospital in Estes Park before dinner. He didn't look forward to it, and if he was late, he didn't care. If he missed it, even better. "Who's without a second now? You or Shan?"

Mac took a seat. He gave the impression of being laid back, at ease, even when he was about to do something risky. Stronger than he looked, Mac edged out Wade in height but not muscle mass. With his ash brown hair getting long, a dilapidated cowboy hat added to the total disregard of appearance. It was a facade.

The exercise room had a magnificent view of the valley. It reminded him of home. "Good question. Both of us," Mac shrugged. It was a non-issue now. Green had worked with him and Shan, and now neither. His position as a pilot was far more important.

"Is that going to be a problem?"

"It's not a concern, no. Cody is there to make certain everyone has a place to fall back to if we need. For any of us to have a second is a waste of time. At least, as far as Gen En issues are concerned."

"Fall back to?" Quinlen repeated. He was aware of the clash of personalities between Wade and Vance, and that Wade didn't trust him.

"It's a defense point for The Vista, and a retreat from all places south and east." He didn't have to say the rest, that it was there for other reasons.

"Are we going to war with Vance?"

"I hope not," Mac chuckled, unconcerned. "We are a few dozen at Cody and they are a lot more." He wasn't afraid of Vance, or the Havens Vance claimed he created. He could imagine factions like The Sixth, vying for control of trade routes. They needed to explore the possibilities.

"Last week, when I was in town, I heard someone say there are ten thousand people in Angelfire." Quinlen spoke low, as if they might be overheard. "That's more than twice the population of The Vista."

"Vance might be an ally. Angelfire could be an ally. Hell, The Sixth, if things go right. There are the things that need to be worked out, and that's my primary focus, finding those allies. I think we've seen a fraction of what life is like out here. I think it's on purpose."

"Sounds familiar. It's going to be an interesting summer."

"It's going to be an interesting summer," Mac agreed. "I have some ideas for Cody. I'd like to get them implemented before the season is over. If you want a promotion," he offered. "I'll have several positions open for ranking officers."

"You're under the impression I want to stay in Cody over the winter."

"Even if you don't, you'll still be in line for a promotion, or retirement." Considering his injuries, Mac would recommend whichever he preferred.

"I haven't decided," Quinlen said.

"Right now, everyone's plans are fluid. We stay here, we go home. We find someplace new." Mac shrugged, shaking his head. "We're never going to learn a thing if we're playing it safe. Wise? Who in the hell knows? Ask me again in a year or two."

"You want to get out here more than any of us, and you're going to go sit in Cody."

"I won't be watching the world go by. Wyoming is a big place."

"Montana, Wyoming, now Colorado. Do we plan on taking over the entire Rocky Mountain region?" He was joking, but Team Three was ambitious and everyone knew it.

"In time." Mac raised an eyebrow. "All in good time. For now, just the places with good beer and rowdy women." Both men laughed. They were young, they couldn't help thinking about women.

"The rest of your team, they're looking for allies, same as you. I thought you'd go together instead of splitting."

"There are three of us. We can cover more ground and be safer doing it. Together, we attract certain attention that we'd like to avoid. I'm not alone in Cody, and Shan won't go out alone either. Wade will. I think it's what he does now."

"I'm surprised she's not insisting on going with him."

"They've already argued. You know Wade wins out."

"Want to go in to town with us later?" Quinlen asked, feeling rested enough.

"I might take you up on that."

"Whatever happens, we've got your back."

Mac didn't imagine he meant his choice of evening entertainment. "Nothing has changed since we left Cody. Don't trust anyone that didn't come out of Montana with us."

"What is this?" Shan, out on the deck, waved her hand at the sparkling lights high in the sky. The men joined her to get a better view.

"Fireworks," Vance said.

"What are we celebrating?" Mac asked.

"Not us," Vance told him. "That's The Sixth, telling us they saw us out and about today." He had invited Team Three for a late meeting, including MacKenzie to be polite, and Shannon because Wade insisted. Late being after dark, and for privacy.

"They use fireworks to taunt you?" Wade could think of better methods of intimidation, but at least it was unique.

"It's their way of saying 'hello'," Vance said. "Are you sending her back as an arbitrator?" he nodded towards Shan.

"No," both her partners answered.

"What if they ask?" she smiled, fooling no one.

"When it's time, I'll be going to visit The Sixth," Wade said, not leaving it up for debate.

"I've got no problem with that," Shan said. She'd like for him to get inside one of their compounds and see what he could see. Two sets of eyes, and such. "But don't speak for me when I'm right here."

They watched the brief fireworks display. "I'm sure our respective governmental bodies will spend many weeks or months working out the details of a treaty. You value your security, and some of you being Altered in hiding adds to that, both good and bad," Vance continued.

"What members of your staff are aware of that aspect?" Wade asked.

"Laine Cooper and JT Caulder. They're my chief advisers. No one else has access to personal information."

JT was Lt. Hunter's younger brother. After a brief reunion, the pair had made their way south to New Mexico. The Caulders were founding members of the place called Angelfire. Phillip, their father, was a senator when there had been a United Southern States. He'd helped author legislation to outlaw the genetic experimentation that created The Altered. The war made it a moot point. Shannon's relationship with Hunter was going to make it relevant again.

"You and Caulder are on good terms." Wade was more aware of their history than he let on. "He knows what you are."

"He knows," Vance admitted. "Believe me, it's been a long road to get his trust, and I'm uncertain that's an accurate assessment of our relationship. We have an understanding. Estes Park and Angelfire are both recognized as Havens. That's why we're acquainted, and work together."

"Business arrangements because of the trade routes all along the Front Range."

"A set of problems not unique, but different from the ones of running a city."

"How long have there been trade routes?" Mac asked. "These trade routes." In his mind, the Rocky Mountains weren't the only place on the planet to harbor survivors. Where there were people, there would be trade. And conflict.

Vance didn't want to start a long conversation so late in the day. "Within a year, scattered groups were making uncoordinated treks across the state. We were south of here, dug in, fighting the elements. A lot of us didn't get another chance, another choice, if we wanted to survive the next winter. It was chaos, even day to day. Moore and Yates went north, thinking it would be easier than dealing with the obvious problems we were having. The Altered were not driven to tolerate each other," Vance said. "The animosity is a learned trait. We weren't raised to make friends. Which makes you two unique, as far as my knowledge of our kind goes."

"Yet you and Rafe established a city," Shan said.

"There were casualties among us. Don't think for a moment we were allies. He claimed his territory, and I let it be to avoid further bloodshed." He led them back to his office, where it was warm and secure from intruders.

"How extensive?" Wade asked, more concerned about border wars than personal problems.

"We started work on clearing the way to an outpost in Cheyenne, Wyoming, two summers ago. Along the Colorado Front Range where it's safe, the West Slope where it's safe, to the New Mexico border." Vance understood they were throwing questions at him to look for untruths, catch him off-guard, find a lie.

"Angelfire is in New Mexico," Shan said, her mind still on The Sixth. She suspected they let her sense a bit of information, that they were there, west of the city, to pique her curiosity. Another reason Vance had moved inside.

"Angelfire is in New Mexico," Vance said. "It's Caulder's stronghold. If you go there, I'd advise you to be prepared."

"Why?" she asked.

"He's witnessed what the most calculating and sociopathic of us are capable of." Vance had, too. "They have strict laws for their protection and peace of mind. You understand that. They fear what The Altered might do. This fear is not unfounded. The routes extend to Nebraska, and we are getting out to Kansas and South Dakota. Caulder has as much at stake in this as we do."

"That's a lot of miles," Mac said.

"Over two thousand miles, including all the places caravans only get to once a year. Most of our activities slow to a crawl after midsummer and stall in the winter."

"How far east is safe?" Wade asked.

"Not far. Oklahoma City is red-lined," Vance told them. "St. Louis is red, and we stay out of Texas. Farther, we don't know. Hardly anyone wanders in from east of the Mississippi these days."

"Texas?"

"They don't have the means to be a danger to us. Texas is a conversation for another day, because it requires other people and several hours. That being said—stay away unless we've had that conversation and you've had time to consider the implications."

Shan raised her eyebrows and shrugged, feigning disinterested. "Too far."

"Texas boundaries now aren't much different from before the war. Angelfire is our most powerful ally, and Texas is a hundred and sixty miles from them. That's a few days on horseback or an hour by airplane. There are reasons to be concerned, so please don't brush it off."

"Understood," she said, meaning it. Texas was a concern, to Vance.

"You'll have to fill me in later on what The Vista has mapped," Vance said.

"Vista Security," Wade corrected. "There are few places, not so complicated as yours."

"Back to the trade routes," Mac urged them, changing the pace of their conversation. As far as he was concerned, it was none of Vance's business what they knew about the north. "You said Moore and Yates took to the north. Maybe Wyoming. We don't want the Cody base infringing on them. How do we make contact?"

"You wait for them," Vance said. "When, or if, they decide they're interested in you, they'll find a way. If you were intruding, you'd know by now. Not like Rafe's response, but Moore is an Altered, so there's that. Yates might as well be. He was a military, a Special Forces officer before the war, and he's spent the past two decades in close company."

"Now you know what you're doing this summer," Wade noted, meaning Mac. "You need to be in Cody."

"It might relieve tensions, in the beginning, if you have Capt. Allen there," Vance said. "Yes, because either of them would be influenced by a woman being present. They'd be less inclined to start a fight over something trivial."

Wade considered it for a moment. "Capt. Allen isn't diplomatic."

"They wouldn't care," Vance said.

Shannon rolled her eyes and snorted a rude comment under her breath.

"Allen and Green are going to be here." Wade had his reasons, ones he didn't plan on explaining. "She's my Scout, my eyes. Cmdr. MacKenzie can handle the situation in Cody. I'd like to get recon sooner rather than later, from outlying areas, as long as it doesn't interfere with your treaties."

"It won't," Vance said. He recognized Wade had already decided about the matter. "I'll have copies of our maps made up for you. When you're making preparations, I'd like to forewarn the way-points."

"Not a problem," Wade said.

"You won't be sitting here, waiting for us to report back?" Shan asked Wade, knowing him better than that.

"Not at all," he said, wanting to make his intent clear to Vance. "I'm going to go see what your acquaintances in The Sixth are up to as soon as the weather breaks."

"You're aware, there are dozens of clans run by The Sixth. The ones that plague me might welcome you, or they might leave you in the mountains to die. Because your team has prior contact doesn't mean as much as you'd think," Vance reasoned. "They protect their own, and as far as they're concerned, you aren't."

"I'm not worried about their reaction to me."

"If that's your decision, I have no authority to stop you." Vance was skeptical. "We're waiting for word from Vista Council. In the meantime, your people are safe here."

"I'd like to get both our airplanes prepped and ready for flight," Mac said. "We're on recall to The Vista. They don't like to be kept waiting." It was a credible story, and a damned good excuse to have a way out fast if they needed to go.

"I understand," Vance said.

"One other thing," Shan said, almost an afterthought. "While Wade is gone, the rest of the team is going to be bored. A handful of us can't overthrow your city. We'd like free access to your public areas."

Vance wondered, if they put their minds to it, how much havoc a handful of them could create.

Chapter Two

Wade swung, connecting with the softball and sent it sailing past the boundary of the baseball diamond into a patch of frozen weeds. A dusting of snow covered the ground earlier, but the wind hadn't started yet.

He motioned for a pitch.

Shan dug another ball out of the duffel bag, shrugging. She didn't have to go find them later. "I thought your shoulder still hurt." They were the only two out, using the field across from the high school complex, where classes were in session. Dressed in long-sleeved tee shirts and jeans, it felt like springtime. They'd left parkas in the vehicle they used when they went to the city.

"When the weather changes," he said, letting the pitch go. It was high and wide. "Nice throw."

"I'm wearing a sidearm," she pointed out, winding up for another pitch.

He smacked it out into the weeds again. "So am I, and mine's bigger than yours." Grinning, he dared her to answer back. They were close friends, and considered each other siblings. He could get away with teasing her.

"You think?"

Leaning on the bat, he stretched carefully. "That one pulled a little."

"So take a break."

"Yeah, we should."

"An impression from our venture out over the blast zone." Shan felt it was important enough to repeat. "Something you need to be aware of, if you aren't already. Cooper dislikes everyone. He dislikes the Altered the most, but he tolerates Vance. Since people here think Cooper's the Big Bad Wolf, it makes me wonder about Vance."

"Agreed. They are not friends, they won't be allies as soon as we've outgrown our usefulness. Which is any time now"

"Agreed."

"Good point, though. Watch Cooper, never turn your back on him."

She nodded.

"Our reinforcements have arrived." He motioned towards the road. Green had flown in earlier with four new officers, and Vance claimed them for a briefing. Now it was Wade's turn. He'd figure out an initiation of some sort for them after the lecture.

Naturally, Shan would play along.

"We are Cody Security first, 'Conda members second, and under no circumstance are we obligated to obey orders from Vance or any other person not part of this group. Vance knows this," Wade said as they made their way to the baseball diamond and congregated at home base. "We will obey their laws, which are more or less the same as ours. If there are questions about our situation, ask."

They lined up, Green standing apart; Chris Taylor, Mitch Elliott, Colin MacKenzie, and Leland. Leland had been eight when the war orphaned him, leaving him with no recollection of his name, or much of anything else. His story wasn't unique.

"They sent me rookies in exchange for Cmdr. MacKenzie."

"They sent you three rookies," Shan agreed, amused. "Mitch Elliott isn't. He's got two years in, if that's any consolation."

Elliott stifled a grin. There would be a point to the hazing.

"Fantastic," Wade said, pacing. "Rookies make rookie mistakes, and here we are. I have to wonder what Mac was thinking." Mac sent him rookies because he'd asked. Vance would have less concern over them. They were trained officers.

"Question," Elliott said.

"Good. What?"

"We're not Vista Security?"

"As long as you're assigned to Cody, no, you're Cody Security. It's semantics, nothing more, but it's important to remember here."

"Your sidearm," Shan held her hand out to Chris Taylor. He checked the safety and handed it to her. She checked to see if it was loaded–it was. "Smith and Wesson .357, 4 inch barrel, custom grip, blued, 6 shot. Do you know why I prefer Sigs?"

"Personal preference. You like big guns. Hell, you used to carry that 10mm Kimber Cmdr. MacKenzie has." He shook his head and smiled, glad to be there. "Being a Scout, because the magazine holds more cartridges. You're the first line of defense for The Vista. In the middle of a firefight, having to stop and reload can get you killed." Chris wasn't reciting what he'd learned in a classroom, he had a handful of months doing real Security work.

"Fairly accurate," Shan said, handing it to him, smiling back. "Also, I like big guns. They tell your opponent how serious you are."

Wade eyed the newest of the group. "Officer MacKenzie. Colin. You have a lot to live up to."

"Yes, sir," Colin answered. His brother was the second youngest commander in Vista Security history.

"Your sidearm."

"I left it with my gear in the Humvee. They said this was a debriefing and maybe a game." Colin knew it was a mistake as soon as Shan asked Chris for his weapon.

"While you're here, never ever go anywhere without at least one weapon on you. Edged, firearm, something," Green said. "That includes the cafeteria, showers, bed, anywhere. If you are lucky, or unlucky enough to be included in a meeting with Vance, and they tell you not to carry, that's the exception."

"Unless I say otherwise," Wade added. "You'll get assignments this evening after dinner. Our quarters are at the military camp on the north side, but we have permission to go where we want, inside the city. Vance's police force keeps track of us. Don't be surprised to notice them around." Wade didn't think he'd have a lot to tell them that Vance hadn't spent three hours on. Green would fill him in on what was said later.

"They follow us?" Leland asked.

"If we had trained and armed strangers traipsing around The Vista, wouldn't you want to be keeping close track of them?"

All four nodded, getting the point.

"I'm going out in the wild soon. When I'm not in contact, the chain of command is Capt. Allen, then Capt. Green. Listen to them, because it's an order, and because they know what they're doing. If we're all gone, Officer Elliott is in charge. He's aware of what to do to keep you busy. You'll get bored, but you'll get over it. Consider it a learning experience. Cody is on call."

"Question," Colin ventured.

"Go ahead."

"Are we safe here?"

"We'll work on the assumption that life here is comparable to The Vista. Keep in mind, we're guests. Be careful what you say in front of others. They act like friends. It doesn't mean they are," Shan said to the group.

"This is all unknown territory. I've been assured the city is secure, and I've seen nothing to say otherwise. Later, we might provide protection for whatever diplomatic officials Council sends," Wade said. They all nodded, silent.

"There are fifteen softballs there," Shan waved towards the out-of-bounds area. "Go pick them up so we can talk about you in private."

Elliott jogged off. The three rookies followed.

"Whatever order they wander back in determines the order of overnight shifts," Wade said. Shan and Green subdued their amusement, knowing they could get added to the roster as easily as not.

"Do you have any concerns about them being here?" Green asked.

He shook his head. "If anyone on my team tells you to get them out, don't ask, just do." Green was aware of the unwritten rule, but it was a force of habit for Wade to say it.

They watched the newcomers scramble around in the weeds for minutes before they came back together.

"Fifteen," Elliott said, dropping the duffel bag.

"They've seen that trick before," Green noted, still amused.

"Capt. Allen, take our rookies to their quarters and get them set up. Green, Elliott and I are going over to the airport and then have a look around the city. We'll be back in time for food," Wade told her. "You know the routine. Give them the tour."

She did. "Who do you want on first watch?"

"Your choice."

"Load up," she told them. "Pretend we have a reason not to be lollygagging around here too much longer." They made their way to the dull gray Humvee parked off the road, next to the winter camo colored one Green drove.

"Stick shift?" Chris asked.

"Automatic," she said, climbing in to the driver's seat. It was on loan from the military base. Estes Park had security concerns, too, and access to more equipment than The Vista.

"I'd like to drive."

"Yeah, not happening. Green, Wade, and I are the only ones allowed to drive."

"It looks standard," Leland said.

"The point is, it's not ours," Shan told them. "Anyway. Estes

Park. You came in on Highway 36 from Lyons, where the airfield and a military camp are. It's well fortified." She pulled a U-turn into the street. "I think they're building another landing strip on the plateau to the north, above the primary base, but don't quote me or repeat that. It might not be common knowledge."

Like The Vista, vehicle usage was limited to officials and emergencies. No regular traffic. "Government offices are in the four story gray building this side of the lakefront. Big Thompson River Road goes through town and is blocked off about three miles east of the city. It's also marked as Highway 34. The river flooded and wiped out most of the road through the canyon a few years after the war and it's never been reopened," Shan recited.

"There's a nuclear power plant right down the road," Chris said. He'd been studying maps for the past four days, since he'd been told he was shipping out. "And my information is dated."

"Forty-five miles east, on the other side of the Continental Divide, and it was closed in 2020."

"Just checking. Massive radiation fields make me a little testy."

"To answer your next question. Rocky Flats is fifty miles south of here, a strike zone, also on the other side of the divide. Yes, I mean a nuclear detonation. We're safe here, concerning that."

"No, thanks."

"It's been surveyed and you can view the video later. We have no reason to be concerned."

"Is this summer going to be long and boring?" Elliott asked to keep things interesting.

"The hospital is at the next intersection. Most of the residential areas are east and south of here." She finished the brief run through town with two more quick turns. "Highway 36 goes up into the mountains." They passed the intersection. "And this way is back to our hotel. There are armed sentry posts on all roads at the city limits and then a mile or two farther out. I've been told they have frequent incursions in the summer. They've had fatalities every year from Scavenger problems, either here or in the outlying villages. Three years ago, a gang burned a farmstead out, killing eleven people and leaving a hundred homeless. Boring enough for you?"

"What's the population here?" Chris asked, trying to memorize everything.

"In the summer, less than eighteen hundred. Right now, fifteen hundred and four people, not counting us. The police force is seventy and the military base has three hundred. Another three thousand people are scattered along the mountains to the west."

"I expected more," Colin added, staring out the window.

"Here, as in Colorado," Shan verified. "There's no accurate count. We know there is a substantial city at Angelfire, which is in New Mexico. Vance hasn't given us details. I don't think he has permission to."

"Really?"

She nodded. "Same drama with different people."

Chris chimed in, "We just changed the scenery. Very little, but a change." He pointed out his window. "What is that?"

A century-and-a-half old motel Vance mentioned in passing, a famous landmark, back in the day, well maintained despite being rarely in use. "They use it for officials from other havens, when they have their meetings here."

"It's the Stanley Hotel," Chris said, sounding like she should have been aware.

"That's what Vance said. I supposed he thought that might mean something to me." It didn't, and she wasn't impressed. Interesting, but not practical.

"It was used in movies. I recognize it."

"I'll ask if you can stay a few nights."

"Oh, hell no," Chris said. "Think horror movies."

Shan had never understood their fascination with old movies, even if there were a few she enjoyed. A lot of officers gathered at the stations during their down time and watched them. They'd even gone so far as to set up a schedule in the winter.

"Okay, then. The Stanley Hotel sits at the north end of Estes

Park. Call for reservations," Leland chimed in, using his best radio voice. The men got the joke and laughed.

"Don't get comfortable," Shan told them. "We're all on-duty until Cmdr. Wade says we're not. Hope he doesn't run us around on night maneuvers until some horrible time long past midnight and then expect us cheery and chipper for breakfast."

"Us?" Chris asked. "As in you and Green, too?"

"There are seven Vistans here, so yes. I mean all of us."

"Ouch," Colin shook his head. "That has to hurt."

"Seven," Chris repeated. "Can I ask something that might be personal?"

"Go ahead," she said, wondering what he could ask.

"Where's Hunter?"

"I'm sure the rumors have gotten around. Hunter is alive and well, and not here. Everything else is classified." That didn't happen often, and she knew it was only going to add fuel to the rumors. Shan went back to their debriefing. "Considering how few we are, we need to stick together," she said, ready to finish up. "Even if it's training we've already done dozens of times. Do you know where The Vista is?"

"North," Colin offered. It reminded her of Mac.

"Eight hundred miles from here," she said. "Cody is four hundred and fifty. Keep that in mind. Any help we call for is that far away." Pulling up to their hotel, she parked in front of the main lobby. Someone would move the Humvee later, before dark. "Last stop. Right now, we're the only people on the second floor. A handful of soldiers will come through a few times a day. Leave them be. They're checking on us. Consider the floor safe, but not private. The doors have locks. My advice is use them."

They headed through the lobby to the stairs. Once they got to their floor, Elliott was waiting for them and gestured to the conference room. "We got called in as soon as you left. Video feed to Cody," he whispered. "They don't sound pleased about the way things are going."

"What things?" Chris asked.

Shan shushed him. "Later," she warned, motioning for them to wait in the corridor, distracted by the unexpected call. Mac had been gone less than a day.

"Apparently, there has been some in-fighting," Elliott said after Shan joined Wade. "I mean Team Three."

"Fighting with who?" Leland asked.

"With whom. Council. Command. Each other."

"About what?"

"Whatever in the hell is going on here. When they should go back to The Vista." Elliott shrugged. "Who knows? I'm not even certain we should unpack."

Shannon discarded her coat and leaned against an overstuffed chair, arms crossed. Wade was pacing while he talked at the screen as Mac looked back. They both wore scowls.

Green kept his distance, waiting near the door where the rookies congregated. "They'll be done in a few minutes," he said, confining them to the hallway. "We'll wait."

"What's going on?" Chris asked anyway, more curious than cautious.

"Nothing to worry about," Green told them. "They work together, and sometimes they yell at each other. Read nothing into it, because it happens. You'll have the same issues after you've been here awhile. The stress level is pretty fucking sky-high. Until one of them says otherwise, it's team business, not ours."

"Secure line?"

"Your brother checked before he left and claimed it was." Kyle Taylor was the closest thing they had to an electronics expert. Mac wanted him in Cody, working on their system. That's where he was, despite his protests.

"Is that why they've scattered? The fighting?" Colin asked.

Green shrugged. "Maybe. Your guess is as good as mine. Again, it'll pass." It was because of Mac. Out of sight, out of mind, and no scrutiny from Vance. "You're aware how they are, how they keep things to themselves. We're told what they have to, in order to keep things moving. This is one of those times."

"So, this is like Station One on alert."

"No," Green almost laughed. "This is like Station Two, if the Council was in charge of us."

"If we're ordered home, we don't have a big damned choice in the matter," Mac said. "An order is an order. Avoiding this isn't going to make it go away."

"For the summer," Wade said. "Because they can call everyone back and if we go running, we'll never find out why they didn't tell us about Estes Park. Vance claims he's never had contact with us before. When he says it, I've got alarms sounding in my brain that say otherwise. We're being lied to from both ends and you're letting them get away with it."

"I'm saying, let's go find out why, from the source, from Command or Council," Mac countered. "Whoever is responsible. Hiding won't get us answers, just more denial. We've been stuck in the cycle all our lives."

Shan didn't like the sound of them fighting. It knotted her stomach and gave her a headache. "Council would've decided, not Command, if it happened over ten years ago. And we're not hiding anywhere. We're going to go see what's out here, if it's safe or not."

"Safe isn't you, Shan," Mac said.

"Things are different now. I almost lost both of you in the last few months," she said. "Priorities change."

"So you're going to go wander the Front Range for Wade and see if you can stir up more trouble?" Mac asked. "That seems like a good idea right now?"

"That's not the plan."

"We need to get our people out of The Vista and out of Estes

Park, move them here, and dig in." Mac shook his head, out of words. "Then the three of us go see Council for answers."

"Council won't give us those answers," Wade said, calmer than Mac. "Not if we go in there, throwing accusations at them. The right questions at the right time."

"They could have warned us."

"A military assassin could be waiting in the next town we explore too, but what's the chance of that happening twice?" Wade asked him.

"What was the chance of it happening once?" Mac came back.

"You want to stay in Cody, you do that. I'm not waiting around for someone else to decide how I live my life, not anymore." Wade was finished arguing the point.

"Stop influencing what she does," Mac said.

"I don't control what she wants to do."

"You tell her what you think is out in the world and then she wants to go look for herself. I've seen you do it, not once or twice, either."

"Shannon, am I ever subtle when I want you to do Scout work?"

Shan straightened up, hands on her hips. "You're not subtle," she told Wade. "And you're not subtle," she directed at Mac. "I'm not subtle. Case closed. I'm not getting in the middle of a pissing contest between the two of you, either. Figure out what we need to do. We've already spent enough time being blind." She stalked out of the room without saying another word.

Mac rubbed his eyes. "We accomplished a hell of a lot today."

Wade gave it a few moments. "We'll check in again on our regular schedule. I have rookies to get through orientation, because I think my logistics officer is out for the rest of the day."

"You think?" Mac asked, angry.

"Don't report any of our issues to The Vista, to Command. Trivial matters," Wade said.

"I tell them what's necessary, and this isn't. She's right, we need to do what we intended all along."

"You have goals there. If you want to switch with Shan, you get to ask her. I'm going, soon."

Mac didn't have to consider it. "Her part of this is safer."

"As much as it can be, I know."

"You wouldn't ask her to be in charge of Cody, anyway."

"That would be Green's job, because I'd want Ballentyne with you. I took months considering this. Do you want to change it now?"

"I don't." He shook his head. "It's a good strategy, but all this change is hard to get used to."

"For all of us. Stay sharp. This will work and move us forward quicker than you expect."

Mac nodded. "I believe you. That fact doesn't make it any easier. Contact us if you need to. Cody Base, out." A moment later, the screen went to gray.

The others had sense enough to keep quiet. Green didn't have that luxury. "You managed to piss them both off."

"It's easier than it looks," Wade offered, unsettled, and having no snap cure for their current disagreement. "Go shadow her, make sure she doesn't get herself in to trouble with Vance. I want to run those flights and we need his cooperation."

Green nodded, taking a hand-held radio off the table as he left.

"This happens when you work with the same people over long periods of time with no break," Wade said to the rookies. "No, it's nothing to worry about. Team Three is Team Three. I hope none of you have an aversion to flying. Scouting here is done by airplane."

None of them did, or at least, no one admitted to it.

"The next handful of days will be hectic until we get used to each other. I haven't decided if I'll ask for another batch of officers, so for now, we'll make do." Wade didn't make quick decisions unless he was under fire. "Overnight watch will be determined by alphabetical order of surnames, four hours each shift, two shifts a night, nine to one, one to five. Capt. Allen isn't included tonight because I don't want her stomping up and down the halls all night, keeping us awake."

"Ah, hell," Elliott figured out he was the one going to be stomping up and down the halls first. The other three laughed.

"Capt. Green will relieve you. Everyone, including me, has a watch."

"Do we have to do this when there's only three or four of us?" Leland asked.

"It's keeping the habit, as actual security concerns are minimal. When a Scout team is out, do it or not. All of you will be aware of how to contact Cmdr. MacKenzie. Also, there's a radio training class tomorrow right after breakfast," Wade told them. "Meet me here. It takes about an hour. After that, I'll have individual assignments."

"We're here to provide support for the scout team," Colin wanted to clarify.

"When you're not being part of the scout team," Wade said. "Listen, learn. You, of all people, should understand the value of choosing your words."

"I do," Colin agreed. Mac had confided in him about the Gen En a year ago, when Colin was deciding if he'd join Security or find a job somewhere else. He'd suspected for a long time. None of them had seen anything that set Team Three apart from other officers, other people. It was unlikely they would soon.

"One meal a day, at midday, is prepared here." Wade continued. They'd be getting hungry soon. Their breakfast had been before daylight. "For other meals, you'll have to find an establishment open downtown. It's less than a mile walk. Or fix your own here. The rooms are cleaned twice a week. You're responsible for your own clothes and bedding. Facilities are on the first floor, north wing. If you request a service, it better be for a good reason, or I'll hear about it later. Use common sense, don't make us look bad. If you need supplies and don't know where to get them, leave a note on your door. Questions?"

"Yes," Colin stepped up and asked what they all were wondering. "Does Command know we're here and not in Cody?"

"The short answer is yes. Beyond that, none of you may discuss this place with any officer that's not here. Cmdr. MacKenzie included that in his departure debriefing. It's worth repeating."

Colin nodded. "There's been a lot of rumors."

"Rumors," Wade said. "It happens, even during Sweeps. Don't waste time on rumors. Do your jobs, let senior officers worry about the rest. Next?"

"Did you nuke the Nomads?" Chris asked, jumping at the chance. He might not get it again.

"Nuke? No, we did not 'nuke' anything. Who said we did?" Wade couldn't think of any way for that rumor to start, not from his people. Not unless one of Vance's advisers was in contact with someone in The Vista.

"Last week Lambert told Mac he'd heard it from Pacifica. He was checking on it. I figured you knew."

"I didn't." If Mac hadn't mentioned it, angry or not, there wasn't a concern. The thing was, information was getting back to The Vista.

"What do we do?" Chris asked.

"Nothing. We won't add speculation to a lie," Wade grimaced. A lie that was too close to the truth to be a coincidence. He'd discuss it with Mac, but not in the conventional way. "Go get settled in to your rooms, your names are on the doors," he told the rookies. He'd be talking to Vance, in person, a lot sooner.

"A spy?" Vance repeated, pouring each of them a double-shot of Kentucky Bourbon. He put the bottle away in the tall oak cupboard behind his desk before he joined Wade on the balcony. They both drank, looking out at the high mountains to the west. Wade had noted there was a large caliber handgun on the shelf that wasn't there before. Vance seldom carried one.

"What I've been told couldn't be misconstrued. My people have nothing to gain from it. Are you in contact with anyone in The Vista I've been unaware of before right now?" Wade wasn't angry. This needed to be dealt with before it became a larger problem.

"No," Vance said. "I can't see what benefit there is to the Estes Park Havens, for your Council to reprimand Team Three."

Reprimand. Not quite what the consequences might be. Command would get them first. "Over the past few years, I've wondered if someone in my circle was reporting to Council. Other than the officers I just sent to Cody, no one there has those details." Wade ran it through his mind, imagining each of them being that spy. "I've got nothing. Shannon doesn't either. Are The Sixth doing this?"

Vance took a deep breath, considering the question. "If they were, again, what would be the point? This is one of your people, passing information for some future benefit. Who has the most to gain from Team Three losing status?"

It was a question he'd consider, but he couldn't see a lie in his words. Hesitation was another matter. "This changes nothing. If you need to know where I am, ask Capt. Allen. It's up to her if she tells you or not. She'll be in charge."

"You're leaving her in my city, in charge of a military force? A teenage girl? I've seen her throwing what amounts to temper tantrums when she doesn't get her way."

"She's not a teenager now," Wade said, smug. "When she gets her mind set on an idea, she makes sure I'm aware. Shan is like me. She knows what she's doing. You don't have to approve, but she's my senior officer here. Her job comes first. A handful of people are hardly a military force."

"Not just like you," Vance pointed out. "We both understand that."

Wade shrugged off the ominous comment. "We'll get a diplomatic party in here as soon as possible. And Shannon, she's not going to do a thing I don't tell her to."

That was what worried Vance the most.

Chapter Three

Green came downstairs early, right after his shift, hoping to get over to the library. Information about the war, the one they called World War Last, but accurately, World War 3, was extensive. They had a decade of pre-war media, censored in The Vista, available to peruse at his leisure. Members of the 'Conda had concluded a long time ago that their archives had been purged. They weren't certain who. Council, Command, or perhaps the original survivors, wanting to forget.

He caught a glimpse of Shan, standing in the dark, staring out the east window of the dining area, and recognized the stance. She was likely seeking out her partners. Sometimes, she had control of her abilities, but more often, a hint of what she was attempting combined with frustration, or something unexpected. The unexpected part was the reason members of Team Three kept their seconds close. Out of their element was forcing change.

He joined her at the window, knowing it wouldn't disturb her.

Outside, it looked like it had been snowing most of the night. "Is Wade out in this?"

"He's out, not in this," she answered after a moment. "No snow south."

Green took that as a good thing, that she could follow his movements, even if not communicating with him. Distance hindered her, not Wade. "Are you awake?" Sometimes, she wasn't.

"Yeah I am," she murmured, shifting, hair loose and uncombed. Civilian clothes, blue jeans, and a long-sleeved button-up shirt. Socks, no boots.

"How long have you been you standing here?" Green asked, not kidding himself into thinking she wasn't armed. She slept with a gun. So did he.

Shan tipped her head a bit. "What time is it?"

"Before seven, but not much."

"A couple hours." She held the faint sensation, hoping it would strengthen into actual contact. It hadn't and wouldn't, now. Wade had started moving, which also meant he was aware of her. Nothing else was necessary. She'd be more at ease to talk to them. This would be sufficient, for now.

"The rest of us will be in for breakfast soon."

She nodded, sleepy. "Give me five."

"You got it." Green suspected she was in contact with Mac as well, with that request. He went in search of coffee.

"Bring me a cup," Shan called. "Please."

He did, half an hour later. The sun was shining, reflecting off the snow, making it look decent out. The rest of the Vistans were out on the veranda, discussing the tactics of being snowbound. She took a seat next to him on the sofa, stretching out. Green was half a foot taller and smirked at her effort to prop her feet up on the table. He kicked back, reaching it with no effort, crossing his arms.

"Shut up," Shan offered.

"Want some advice on what to do with them?" he asked, meaning the rest of their team. "Because if you're this restless, you better know they're getting to that point."

She nodded. "Go ahead."

"Forget all this security protocol. The city is safe."

"A gateway city. You know how I feel about its inhabitants."

He agreed, "I do. A gateway city. One that's maintained by Vance, and we've both heard him being called 'Governor' more than a few times. He's keeping several thousand people scattered clear across the state, reasonably safe. I think we'll be fine here, if we're pacing the floors worrying about what his ulterior motives are or not. If he wanted us dead, we'd already be there."

"When I was wandering around out here last summer, during Sweeps, the old man that owned the farm where we stayed called him Governor Vance. I didn't think he was serious."

"Apparently he was. We can use the time for something constructive, more than flying around and looking at the scenery."

"What did you have in mind?"

"I don't want to mess with orders you have from Wade, Mac, and Command. We need to push forward, get out there, and see what we can see. That's been a priority, and this is our chance. Every one of you, of Team Three, has said The Vista will have diplomats all over this place, and soon. If we don't scout now, we're going to miss the opportunity."

"My orders from Command are to get out there and scout. You already know the routine: half day jaunts a few miles around here, sometimes on horses, and on great days, we get to fly."

"Does that sound even a little like what they've been doing all along? Giving you chores to do, sending you out where they know nothing is, to keep you occupied."

"It sounds exactly like that."

"Now you know. I'm surprised you didn't see it before."

"I had other concerns. Command doesn't want me scouting alone. Wade out and out forbade it." Shan raised one brow, recalling the conversation going from serious to ridiculous just that fast.

"Forbade?" Green repeated, trying to imagine it.

"He said 'I forbid you to go off by yourself, out of the city, for any amount of time.' Then he had words about The Sixth, and some of them were, well, bad. Wade uttered swear words." The thing about it, Wade rarely swore.

"Bullshit," Green challenged, teasing her.

"Would I lie?"

"I can't imagine why. You have to admit, Wade swearing is pretty fucking unusual."

"It damned sure is," she agreed. They could mock his speech patterns all they wanted. Wade was hundreds of miles away. Of course, they'd do the same thing if he was sitting there with them.

"Three of us go, three of us sit here. Short expeditions of a week or less when we take the airplane out," Green got back on track.

"Keep it to five days, maximum." She suspected Wade's orders could change without warning.

"Set up an arrangement with Vance."

"You're the only pilot we have. I don't think you have to worry about getting left here too often," Shan said. "You need time off, too. You'll be the senior officer out there when I stay here, too."

"There's that. I worry you'll be off, walking across half the state if you think you missed something," he smirked. She had tried that, right after Wade had headed for Colorado on his own. It hadn't worked out well.

"I told you to shut up, didn't I?" Shan had learned a long time ago she could confide in him. He was easy to talk to, easy to joke with.

"You did."

"Good," she said. "I'll get permission and pick a day when the weather looks good. You, Elliott, and MacKenzie get to go see what's south of here. Draw up a flight plan, get me a copy. Don't use more than a quarter tank of fuel one way. Or whatever is safe. You know more about airplanes than I do."

"Short and simple," he recited.

"Yes, until I get a better feel for this place."

"We've been here five months."

"Has it been that long?" Shan asked, furrowing her brow.

"It's almost April," Green said.

She considered it. "Damn." Springtime.

"You hate it here."

"Hate is a powerful word."

"You have a strong dislike of this place."

"True."

"Homesick?"

"If I thought about it a lot, I suppose I would be. Which is crazy, because we figured we'd be out for two or three years when we got the Cody base."

"Plan all you want. Until you act, you can only guess how you're going to feel. I don't care how much Team Three plots out every tiny detail, and how you insist you're different, you're still human and there are still human variables. You miss your parents, your friends, and that's natural."

The rookies wandered in, shaking off the snow and cold.

"I miss a lot of things," Shan confessed. "Hell, I miss driving circles around The Vista. That doesn't mean I'm ready to go back. We've got too much to do here to make the Cody base viable and safe."

"I hoped that was still our aim," Green said.

"What's our aim?" Elliott asked.

"Getting Cody squared away," Shan said. "I told you not to get comfortable. We're all going to get a lot of flight time and more scout time in the next month. Don't expect a regular schedule."

"This isn't The Vista," Green finished up for her. "Can I ask you something?"

"Always."

"Don't lie to me about it." He glanced around to see the rookies were out of earshot. They were more interested in who was stuck cooking breakfast.

Shan nodded.

"Was that fight the day the rookies got here real?"

"I said I wouldn't lie to you, so I can't answer that."

"I was with the team before you, Shan. You don't get to keep secrets from me, and I deserve to know."

"Yeah, you do." She rubbed her eyes. "It got out-of-hand. We started out pretending to fight and then it got real."

"That's what I thought. Try not to worry about it."

"It'll pass," she said. "We've had disagreements before. I'm not as worried about it as you are. It was in the heat of the moment, and it's over now."

Green was aware. In The Vista, most of their careful planning had been to avoid having their abilities discovered. They were free of that stigma now, looking for answers to the same old questions. One of those questions was if the war had happened because of them, because of their kind. The Gen Ens, the genetically enhanced, The Altered. Another, how long had The Vista Council and Security Command known about the Havens, and did they ever plan on telling the citizens. There were others, most being simple things. The answers wouldn't be simple.

~You knew Command had nothing to do with Wade going to Colorado,~ Mac said first, a statement rather than a question.

In the back of his thoughts, it was a question. Shannon could sense it. ~I never asked,~ she said. ~Sometimes, it's better to shut up and observe rather than accuse, since I'm the most junior member of Command. There are issues they don't discuss with me. With us.~

~I didn't ask, and I won't until I can talk to him.~

~Good idea. So talk.~ Shan was in Estes Park and it was past midnight, again. She was pacing the floor of her quarters.

Mac was asleep in his apartment in Cody. She could taste the Scotch he'd medicated himself with, enhancing the Gen En effect.

Wade was far from sleep and not alone, somewhere in central Colorado.

~Ask him,~ she repeated, drawing Mac's focus. That was the difficult thing, getting focus where all of them could communicate. For a few moments, there was fog and confusion. Wade drew them together, a bright pinpoint of that focus they lacked.

It dissolved, leaving Team Three sitting together in the dayroom of Station Two. ~It's easier to visualize something you're familiar with,~ Wade explained, sipping coffee from a chipped ceramic cup. They sat across from him, minus coffee or any other sort of libation. Just as well, considering. It would be another distraction.

~But you're having coffee,~ Mac pointed out. ~I can smell it.~

~Yes, now. I was about to engage in more personal activities.~

~Thanks, but information I did not need,~ Shan said, tension in her thoughts obvious. Emotions bled over between the trio. Wade had been cautious in the first years when Shan had exhibited her similarity in abilities. She was too young to understand those emotions. Ten years on, she understood, and could avoid them when she had forewarning.

~Unintentional, and not what you think,~ Wade offered.

She'd misunderstood for a moment. Whoever his company was, they were concealed for their safety and nothing else.

~Have you had any sort of contact with Security Command since July?~ Mac got right to his concerns. It was a more civil conversation than their last one.

~Not directly. I have standing orders.~

~You didn't have permission to go to Colorado. That's why Shannon went after you, that's why you gave conflicting orders to keep her away.~

~That's not entirely accurate.~

~Accurate enough.~

~No,~ Wade disagreed. ~Technically, it's about twenty-five percent accurate, but details now are a moot point.~

~If we ever get to be old and gray, tell me what twenty-five percent I was right about.~ Mac wasn't angry, he was confused, and had been since July.

~I will,~ Wade said. ~What are we doing here?~

~My fault,~ Shannon said. ~There was boredom, and I got to thinking how the team should be together. You left me here. It's because I'm female and almost every other person in Command is not. You two still feel the need to protect me. After what happened with Rafe, I'd think you'd know I can take care of myself.~

Rafe had told her several of the corporations creating The Altered planned to use them exactly the way Vance had used him—to control the population after the war. They hadn't foreseen the minor war they instigated would domino into a worldwide event.

~What happened with Rafe is why we want to protect you,~ Mac said.

~We were close to losing that battle,~ Wade agreed. ~I'd like you to stay in Estes Park. I don't expect you will, no matter what our reasoning. Even if we make it a Command order, it's a simple thing for you to work around it.~

~I have no intention of 'working around' whatever orders I get,~ she told them. ~I have plans, too.~

~You think you want to go back to The Vista when it gets towards autumn,~ Wade sensed. ~Shan, you know what they're going to do when we go back?~

~I do.~ They'd had long discussions about it, in January, when Shan and Wade were in the hospital recovering from the offense against Rafe. They were looking at serious reprimands, certainly. Maybe even career-ending ones. They'd known the risk before they moved against him.

~We'll deal with that when the time comes. This autumn, next year, whenever,~ Mac said, suggesting that they had more pressing concerns.

~Right now,~ Wade said, avoiding an argument. ~We all have orders from Command. Different orders. I've been with them the longest, and I have to think those are carefully constructed orders and not meant to be discussed.~

~I concur,~ Mac agreed, not liking the secrecy and not having a choice about it. He'd been plotting with Command almost as long as Wade.

~Good call, filtering information getting back to The Vista,~ Wade told him.

~With you out of contact again, there wasn't much of a choice. Why did you leave Estes Park?~ Mac asked, not finished yet.

~Vance has never given us anything. We know next to nothing about him, Estes Park, or even what his status with Rafe was, in January. He's keeping us from asking the questions we need to ask. I'm looking for another source.~

~The Sixth,~ Shan filled in. ~You're in Jacob's town.~

~I'm close, I will be soon. We need to learn about these safe havens, too, from whatever council or office that handles it,~ Wade said. ~This is our one chance, one time we don't have someone looking over our shoulder to see what we see, and censor what we hear.~

~We'll find out.~ Mac was more optimistic. ~Those allies we're moving towards are closer now.~

~They've made it pretty clear they prefer us to be isolated. Will Council even cooperate?~ Shan asked.

~We aren't certain of the reasoning behind that,~ Wade pointed out. ~When Command offers Council evidence of everything we've found, they can't ignore it, not anymore. If the stalemate goes on, we can assume they're both hiding the facts.~

~Another reason to go home,~ she said, fidgeting.

~We will. Just not yet,~ Wade assured her. ~If The Vista bows out, there's Cody. It will take time for us to get organized. This is what we need to do, for Cody and The Vista, even if they don't see eye-to-eye with us.~

~What if Council tells us we can't create our own affiliations?~ Mac asked.

~Outside the boundaries of The Vista, outside the inner perimeter, Council has little or no authority. Neither does Command.~ Wade told them, and waited for their reactions.

~Are you sure?~ Mac asked.

~It's been tested with minor cases, with the Ranchland satellites. If Council wants to challenge us in Cody, they're more than welcome to.~

~What we're doing now, it's more risky than what we did in January,~ Mac said.

~You're right.~

~We've had no proper preparation for this,~ Shan said.

~More than you imagine. We go out into the world, we find other people. Decide what we want, without others telling us.~

~Hope for a little good luck,~ Mac added, knowing Wade's disdain of the word.

~Luck?~ Wade repeated.

~Yeah, yeah,~ Mac said. ~You don't believe in luck. A year ago, you didn't believe there were cities scattered across the country, either.~

~That's not my point. I'm going to go find those places we only imagine exist. I don't have to have permission from anyone and neither do you. We're not prisoners. If you aren't afraid of Council, or Command, you should do the same thing,~ Wade challenged.

~I've got Cody to run, because you dropped that job on me when you left,~ Mac said. ~Priorities.~

~Damned right,~ Shan added.

~I'll understand whatever decision you make, but I've already made mine. Watch your backs, always,~ Wade got the last word in, as usual, their contact breaking into three distinct parts before it faded away.

"You have our flight plans and a working schedule," Green told them. "We'll be in unknown territory. Those are cursory plans. When we have the ability, we'll radio in at dark." The Vistans stood in the hangar, an informal meeting the only orders they'd have for a week.

Shan had already spent an hour re-evaluating her pack. They had weight limits on their supplies. Guns and ammo were heavy. So were food and water. There wasn't room for a lot of extras between her, Green, and Colin.

The first leg of their journey was three hundred miles south. Vance had pointed them to a fuel depot and supply cache on the Colorado side of the old state line with New Mexico. The last jump, another two hundred miles south. The havens had a way station they called West Mesa, perhaps not ironically, just west of a place called Albuquerque. That was their destination.

Vance claimed the weather wasn't warmer, six hundred miles south.

"If we fail to call in, don't panic. We've been over this." Shannon didn't enjoy lecturing them because it annoyed the hell out of her when senior officers treated her like she'd forget as soon as they were gone. These rookies were no different. "Call Cody, and if they do anything, it'll be to move you back there, so keep that in mind."

"You wouldn't leave us here if there was an imminent threat," Elliott reasoned.

Shannon rolled her eyes and snorted. "You're right, but don't assume things like that. I'll tell you about the week I got transferred from training to a rookie one of these days."

"During the last Blackout. I remember you burned down Depot South."

She looked shocked. "I did not burn down anything. Nomads firebombed it when I happened to be there." They all laughed. She wasn't offended. The Blackout had been a deadly lesson, though.

"Yeah," Green confirmed. "We ran like scared deer."

"I remember thirty of them," Shan added. "And two of us. Point is, you have a backup plan. We didn't."

"We do," Elliott acknowledged. "Don't panic. Sit back and keep an eye on things. Watch and listen. Wait by the radio for you to call in, maybe."

"Yes," Green said. "Enjoy the free time. Try not to burn the city down."

"You're lucky to be our only pilot," Shan said, laughing. "Or you'd be sitting in the radio room for the next week."

"Time to go." He didn't like filing reports with Vance and tried not to follow the schedule. It felt safer.

"What's so interesting in West Mesa?" Colin asked, half an hour into the flight.

"We're watching Nomads, for now. Out of the range of the havens. Vance doesn't have much to say about it. Shan is looking for The Sixth," Green told him. "Certain people involved with The Sixth."

"Vance said Moore and Yates went north," Shan said. "He also insinuated either or both might not be alive now. I don't trust either assumption. So, we're looking south first."

"Seems reasonable to me," Colin said.

"We're also waiting for Wade to do something," she added, sitting back, eyes closed.

"I've been hearing you, and my brother, and Kyle Taylor say that for years. Are you ever going to do something you want?"

"Good point," Green said, giving her a sideways look. Touchy subject.

Shannon didn't have a snide remark. "I think that's why all of us are going our own way now. Sure, it's Security issues and Command orders, but there's more to it. I don't understand why Wade left me with Vance, because we don't get along well and we never will."

"He knew that, and he knows you enough to predict what's next," Green said. "You'll find The Sixth before he does, or you'll go to

Cody and be second in command. Better yet, what you do best–come up with an alternative none of us can see until you see it. That's how we finally found The Sixth."

"Finally?"

"They've been watching us, or the Gen En among us, for years. In some cases, since before the war," Shan said.

"That's kind of creepy."

"You don't have to tell me. I've spent fifteen years thinking that."

"What do you think you'll do now?"

"I've been considering my options for months. We're moving south for a specific reason as well."

"What's in the south?"

"Angelfire," Green said. "If Vance isn't eluding, that's where the seat of power is for the havens. The assembly there has a say over everything south of Cody, into Colorado and a bit of New Mexico."

"Including Vance?"

"Oh, yes, especially Vance."

"We don't need more enemies," Shan said. "Especially ones we're unaware of. We make contact, we play by their rules because this isn't The Vista, and maybe we learn a few things about the world. Concentrate on establishing trade routes. Help where we can. If the Gen En aren't acceptable, we send someone else. There has to be a hierarchy of The Altered in all the clans of The Sixth we've heard about. We're being led away from that, on purpose."

"Did you ever think we were alone?" Colin asked.

"The Vista? No. Even after hearing for years in school, it never made sense. I was right, but that doesn't change the fact that Council would rather we be in the dark. Be alone."

"It saved everyone there, right after the war," Colin pointed out. "Why do they want to stay that way?"

"It's at least partially because of us," Shan said.

"You never said what The Sixth told you," Green reminded her. "A clue would be nice."

"It doesn't need repeating."

"When your safety is at risk," Green was serious. "That's part of my job, a big part."

"It's politics, and I hate getting involved in that. Let me do my job." Shan sat up, wrinkling her nose and continuing on. "Yes, there were groups that said we weren't human, and it scared them. The biotechs that helped create the Gen Ens were made illegal in places. Parts of what was the United States included. They never got around to deciding what was next, because until just before the war, few people even knew we existed."

"What was Rafe,?" Colin asked.

"A Sixth, but more, a sociopath created to do just what he was still doing twenty years after–hunting down and killing other Gen Ens. Altereds," she corrected herself.

"Why?"

"Long and complicated," Shan told him. "The past is gone. Let it be."

"It's not over," Green said. "If it was, none of us would be in Colorado, looking for answers."

"Another day like today, and we'll be in sight of Sheridan," Lambert decided, tucking a folded map away in his parka. It was a slight exaggeration.

Snow still covered the high peaks, but spring was showing in distinct ways. Trees were budding and creeks overflowing from the thaw. Their path east narrowed into the mountains, still treacherous from ice lingering in the deep shadows.

"Since we're tracking Nomads at a not-so-discreet distance, it looks like the perfect setup for an ambush. Their home, their call." Quinlen added his opinion, knowing Mac wouldn't have invited him along if he didn't want it.

"I agree," Mac said. "We'll head home to Cody tomorrow before daybreak. Tonight we camp back a couple miles in that roadside park." It was the second time in a week a group of riders had gotten close enough for them to take note. While he didn't believe they were The Sixth, he thought it merited closer attention. The riders, however, were uncooperative, disappearing into the landscape. It reminded him of Scouts in The Vista, leading travelers away from the city.

"Instead of going right to our routine, we should get a few people out in the east valley, five or ten miles. Do some scouting. We've done little outside of town," Lambert said. "As in none."

"We've been busy, but we should add that to the top of the list," Mac agreed. "I'd like for us to know Cody as well as we know The Vista, by the end of the season."

"When are you going to tell me why I'm here? I was in charge of the 'Conda and now I'm in Cody, replacing Taylor," Lambert asked, getting the idea no one was going to bring up those questions, the ones Mac had been avoiding. He'd been there a week, and nothing.

"You're here to replace Taylor."

"I said that first. Why?"

"Multiple reasons. He doesn't approve of me being in charge of Cody. He doesn't approve of Wade and Shan staying in Colorado, and doesn't want to be out here with those things all being facts."

"Has he dropped out of the 'Conda?"

"No, not even close. Taylor is running the 'Conda for now. The majority of members are in Cody, or will be soon. I'd rather be with my team, seeing the world. For now, that's not possible. We need Cody to be self-sufficient. It will take us two years."

"Is that possible?" Quinlen asked.

"Yes," Mac said. "We have the groundwork in place. I can't keep leaving Ballentyne in charge, either, because it's not his responsibility. It's mine."

"Go join your team," Lambert said. "It's what you're supposed to be doing out here. It's what Command has been setting you up to do since you joined Security."

"Who claimed to know what Command wants?"

"When Wade recruited me to help organize the 'Conda, he also recruited me to help organize Team Three. A lot of issues have been discussed."

"About the same time they appointed me to Command," Mac figured.

"Is everyone in Command?" Quinlen asked.

"Everyone in Team Three. There are nineteen actual members now. Sometimes there are a few more, not less usually, and always an odd number to avoid voting ties. They also have various advisors."

"You should be in Colorado," Lambert repeated.

Mac shook his head. "We attract too much attention when we're together. The Gen En gravitate towards each other, but it ends badly for everyone concerned. Until we have the means to defend ourselves, we're safer apart."

"What really happened in January?" He'd read the official reports, and knew fiction when he saw it.

"Rafe. He was Gen En and had watched us for years. Wade and Shan. I'm different enough to be invisible, to a point. If I go out there again, that might change."

"He was your target?"

"Yeah."

"Maybe being invisible is your superpower."

"Ouch," Mac grimaced, deadpanning. They were bored, tired, and cold. Part of the job.

"Don't take it personal."

"Don't repeat that to anyone, ever."

"No problem," Lambert grinned, and all three laughed.

"He launched the warhead that ended up on the Missouri Breaks," Mac told them. "We saw it, because Shan saw it."

"I'd heard that last part," Lambert confessed. "How are The Sixth involved in all of this?"

Mac considered what to tell them, watching the trail as the horses made their way through the broken rock and intruding underbrush. All Rafe had revealed was that The Sixth existed and were an unknown factor. Vance hadn't told them anything. What they guessed was because of Shan's brief encounter with The Sixth, prior to their offensive in Manitou. "Ask me again when I know something."

"I will. What in the hell is Wade doing?" Lambert didn't pull any punches. He'd been with them for too long.

"Wade has gone out of contact to keep the rest of his team, including us and everyone in Estes Park, from more trouble later. Officials in The Vista might decide we are operating beyond our authority."

"Good excuse," Lambert said.

"He always comes up with those," Quinlen said. "This time, I have to agree. We need to find out who we can trust."

"You two have the advantage of knowing what happened, as opposed to the reports I've read." Lambert let it go at that. A lie was a lie, and if they'd all agreed to it, there was a good reason.

"As far as you're concerned, every word is true," Mac told him.

"You don't want to fucking know," Quinlen said. They'd lost his partner and another officer. The wounded included Wade, Shan, and Quinlen.

Lambert believed them.

"For now, our priorities are to keep working on getting Cody running, keeping the immediate area secure–and yes, that's going to include getting a Scout schedule set up. The other project is to get the road to The Vista as cleared and safe as a handful of people can with three hundred miles of work."

"What route are we using?" Quinlen asked.

"Highway 14 through Yellowstone, 287 north to the interstate. After that, the rest will be easy."

"Three hundred miles," Lambert repeated.

"As we get supplies, I want to set up caches every forty or fifty miles, especially up in the mountains because there won't be winter travel there, no matter how good a job we do."

"Is this a break from The Vista, then?"

"No, of course not," Mac said. "In the end, we're doing this to keep them safe. We have a tiny clue about what's out here, and the base is more important because of it."

"You're poking the bear," Lambert said.

"I'm doing what they trained me to do. When they let us out of the valley, they knew what to expect. Don't blame me because they've had second thoughts."

Chapter Four

West Mesa, New Mexico nightfall April 10

"As long as we keep the fire small, we shouldn't attract attention," Green said, straightening the canvas and snapping it closed. "Grab that."

Shan caught the tent pole and pulled it in to place. Smaller than the ones they used during Sweeps, sturdy, warm, and winter camo in color. Perfect for their current surroundings. It was her second trip, Green's third, and Chris' first to the cache.

Landing at the tiny airstrip near the top of the plateau before dark, they had pushed the plane into a secured hangar, or as secure as possible, in the middle of nowhere. The hike was about a mile and a half downhill, to the gully picked to camp at on their previous trip. It was sheltered from the wind and out of sight. The terrain, rough in places, covered in sage, mesquite, and sand, with scattered areas where housing subdivisions had existed. Foundations and debris were all that remained.

"Are we digging into the supplies or catching our own?" Chris asked, meaning dinner.

"Getting late to go hunting," Shan said. "Break out the dehydrated rations. They aren't tasty, but they are food. Sort of." They'd hauled five hundred pounds of supplies in two trips, buried nearby and marked so other Vistans would recognize them.

"The creek water was safe last week," Green baited the rookie.

"Check the water supply every time," Chris said.

Shannon smirked at Green. "He trained with me."

"For an entire month."

"Hey, I'm right here," Chris said.

"We don't have unwanted company, but I'm going to look at the city anyway." Discarding her thermal face-mask and hat, Shan walked up the slope to overlook the valley.

Both men followed. Chris had no clue what to expect, but Green did and had the snap on his sidearm undone. The city could have been any metroplex or village on the continent. Long abandoned but for Scavengers and occasional Nomads. There were burned out areas, entire sections blockaded, and neighborhoods untouched except by twenty years of time. This city was Albuquerque, half a million people at the onset of the war. Currently, the population was three.

As far as Green cared, dozens of Scavengers were ready to make a run at their position. He went along prepared.

"Relax," she said, holding a hand up to feel the breeze. "The area is clear."

Green had no intention of relaxing. "What's going on?"

"Concerning what?"

Fair warning. "You can tell me what you see."

"Of course I can. Nothing is moving tonight."

"Then why are we here?"

She wrinkled her nose, closing her eyes. "I'm learning to focus. People."

"Close?"

"No, not to us." She shifted from one foot to the other, dark hair fluttering in the breeze. "They're in the past, anyway. *Povernite tank vokrug.*" Shan blinked, glancing at Green. "*Net? Povernit' tank navkolo.*"

"What does that mean?" Chris couldn't hold back the question. He had a few more, a lot more, if they let him ask.

"No clue," Green said. "Ghosts. All I can swear to is that it's not English or Siksika."

"By the time they got their orders, the ICBMs were already inbound," Shan announced, sounding like she was reading to them. "A few headed for their assigned target. Most of them turned south and didn't stop until they crossed the equator."

"Who went south?" Green asked.

Shan looked around, shaking her head. "The soldiers? There were a couple of airbases. Probably across the dotted line in Texas, and we better not go to Texas. They were too late to help. They're somewhere in South America now."

"No shit?" Chris said. "You saw that just now?"

Saving him from a lecture, Shan walked back towards camp. "I didn't 'see' it. That's not an accurate word. There isn't a way to explain the ability, as far as I know. I felt it, I could hear it, visualize it, all rolled up in one sensation. I was there."

"Like I said, ghosts," Green added. "What were they saying?"

"Something about tanks. I don't know what language, but I think it was more than one. They were confused. After all this time, it doesn't mean much to us."

"Foreign troops, though."

"Yeah. Allied military units trained at bases here. On this continent, I mean," she told them.

"Not in Montana."

"I have no idea. Back to current events. A fair sized airport, over to the southeast," she said. "Military. Maybe ten miles, but less, I think."

"On the map. Vance said there was nothing interesting. Cleaned out years ago." Green shrugged. "We can fly over on the way back, or take a hike in the morning."

"Remind me."

"Great," Green said, seeing she was done with the subject. "Start that fire and we'll eat early, sleep early and be on the road early."

"You're turning 'early' in to a four-letter-word," she decided. "I haven't slept in late since June."

"If you're looking for sympathy," Green regarded her.

"Just stating a fact."

"Do we ever take an assignment serious?" Chris asked.

"There's no team, no officer, more serious than they are," Green said. "In a year, you'll understand. Right now, learn to roll with it, or you'll be back at the ranches, up to your knees in cow shit."

"I guarantee you, Mac would prefer it that way. My only advice is, do what you want, not what he thinks is best," Shan spoke from experience.

"Don't take advice from other officers."

"You're both offering me career advice," Chris said.

"Exactly," Shan said. "Now you understand. The only opinion that matters is your own. If you want to go back to The Vista, go. Security, ranches, caravans, doesn't matter."

"I wish you could hear your own lecture," Green told her.

"I never take my own advice."

"None of you do. You can dish it out, but when it comes time to do as you say, it's like talking to a brick wall." Green caught himself talking with his hands and stuffed them in his pockets.

"I might be insulted," Shan said.

"No, you aren't. The three of you are too damned smart to be wasting away in Security. You're some of the smartest people in The Vista." Green knew it was true because he knew them, and more than a few people had said it over the years. "You've confined yourselves to Security and you're missing out on a lot of opportunities because of that tunnel vision. Wade knows, and I think he's making the break all of you need to make. You need to pay attention. Someday, you'll thank him."

"Did you get any sleep?" Chris asked, hiking with Shan along a broken blacktop that led into the base. They'd started out two hours earlier, after daybreak, to have a look around. "I didn't mean to cause a fight."

Shan snorted in amusement. "That wasn't a fight. That was expressing opinions. Everyone is allowed an opinion."

Green kept behind them a discreet distance and off the road, hidden in the treeline. The area had plenty of cover, as if no human had ventured there in years. It would be a short day, getting video if they found anything interesting. They'd be back to the hangar before dark.

"I don't sleep a lot during these sorts of scouting trips," she said. "It's normal for me. When I do rest, it's in the middle of the day."

"Gen Ens tend to be night owls," Green interpreted, catching up a bit as they approached the west gate.

"Even the ones that don't know?" Chris asked.

"I won't tell you anything about them. This is what we know about Team Three," Shan said, slowing down to let him catch up. "Too much hiking for you, rookie?"

"Tired," Chris confessed. "It's been a long week."

It was Green's turn to make a sarcastic comment. "Every week, all summer, is long. The schedule will be erratic and your duty will break your regular life into pieces." He gestured he was moving on ahead while they rested. "Shout out if you need help." The ten-foot high fencing seemed intact. He slung the AK on his back and strapped it down before scaling the fence.

"Do we have to climb the fence?" Chris asked.

Shan shook her head. Green disappeared behind the gatehouse.

A few moments later, he reappeared and pulled the gate open, casually leaning on the fence and looking bored.

"He unlocked it. Sometimes we climb the fence, sometimes we drive a truck through it. Today, we walk in." Shan headed off to join Green. "Showoff," she called, shaking her head.

"From the looks of the place, nothing happened here," Green reported as they joined him. "No cars, no debris. Some places were in lockdown early on, thinking they'd be back to work in a few weeks, after the flu season passed." So many places seemed as if humans had simply disappeared.

"Colorado Springs was intact, for the most part." Shan grimaced at the memory. Their inadvertent intrusion on Rafe's home had set in motion the events that led them to Estes Park, and now, New Mexico.

"My recommendation is a quick scout in cover. If there are inhabitants, we'll see signs of them. Otherwise, the military moved out of here and no one has bothered to burn the place down in the meantime."

"Did the flu turn people into pyromaniacs?" Chris wondered. Almost every city or town he'd seen showed evidence of massive fires.

"Not at all," Green laughed. "Accidental fires. As the electrical grid failed, emergency services were overloaded, and then they were gone. Once a fire started, it burned until nature put it out."

"Some of them were on purpose," Shan added. "Not en mass."

They'd hiked about a mile north before Chris stopped, waved them off, and went to be sick in the ditch.

"Weren't you ill yesterday?" Green asked Shan.

"Motion sickness. It stops as soon as I hit solid ground."

"I suppose this calls for a preliminary exam," Green decided, being the only Vistan in two states that was a medic. "That's as good a place as any," he indicated a gray building across the road.

"I'll stand here."

Fifteen minutes later, he rejoined her outside. "That was pretty inconclusive. He's got a low grade fever and mild nausea. Other than that, I can't even guess. He could have motion sickness, a virus. Hell, our rations could be going bad. My opinion, we should get back to the camp and see how he feels in the morning."

"All right," she said as Chris returned. "Let's head back. I've got point because we're using the main road this time. We'll try again tomorrow, if everyone's up to it."

In the three hours it took them to hike back, Chris was sick several times and his fever started an upward trend. He went to his bedroll while Shan and Green set up the smaller tent. It was threatening rain.

"He's not in quarantine, because that would be a waste of time," Shan was talking to herself. "I don't want to be that close if he's sick again. Barfing noises make me want to join in."

"Ye of the weak stomach," Green offered. "I understand. I'll take the first watch. Rations at dark, you get a watch, we decide what to do after I reevaluate then, around midnight."

"As good a plan as any. I'm going to sleep, maybe. If it rains, don't stand out there in it."

———

It was after dark; it was drizzling, cold, and Shan was aware she wasn't getting a weather report when Green came in. "What is it?"

"Chris. My best guess would be appendicitis."

With her mother being a surgeon, she understood the implications of their situation. "Options?" Rolling out of her sleeping bag, she started gathering her gear.

"We can wait until daylight and beeline for Estes Park. That's a lot of hours to hope he doesn't go critical. I can't do a damned thing here, but there's the option of attempting an evac now. I can't guarantee I'll be able to fly in the ice and the wind, in the dark, hell, even in the light. We have the radio, so we could send a mayday to Vance and hope they pick it up."

Shan finished dressing, rubbing her eyes, assessing. "What are the chances his condition won't change for twelve or fifteen hours until we can get him to a hospital?"

"Not great."

"If he gets worse?"

"The pain will increase." He skipped details, knowing full well she'd ask if she wanted that information. Medical things sent her way out of her comfort zone, all because of her mother being a doctor. She'd witnessed some horrifying incidents, early on after the war, at the hospital in The Vista.

"I'll try the radio," she decided.

"You know where I am."

"Lyons Airfield, this is Cody Air One, over," Shan tried first. The radio station was in Estes Park, while the airstrip was twenty miles east, on the edge of the mountains. There was only static. She tried the secondary frequency, with the same results. After a few more tries, she paused, attempting to see if either of her partners was within reach. Neither had been for some days, and still weren't.

She tried for a long shot, changing frequencies. "Cody Home Base, this is Cody Air One, over." Static. With a sigh, she grabbed her parka and went off to see how they were faring.

"The storm looks like it's breaking up," Green said, holding the tent flap for her.

"Good. Is he asleep?"

"No," Chris answered. "Just trying to rest a little and not move around so much."

"It's a mile uphill to the hangar," Shan reminded them.

"Did we get an answer?" Green asked.

"No. I think we should get up there and stay until daybreak, or until you say we need to go. One tent and a heater will keep us from freezing. Everything else is replaceable. Taylor is not."

He considered it. "Break down the smaller tent. You pack it, I'll get him ready. It's going to be dark by the time we get there."

"I can see at night pretty well."

"I remember," Green said. "Let's do this."

The trek was slow, with Chris stopping to rest every few steps and refusing help. They crested the slope, and all three sat down to catch their breath.

"I need to prep the plane," Green said after a few.

"It's getting damned cold," Chris said, shivering.

Shan and Green exchanged looks. "It's cold enough," she agreed. "You're going to sit in the hangar while I play lookout and Green gets the Cessna fueled. The latest we'll be in the air is daybreak, sooner if either of us says so."

"How serious are you about going now?" Green asked a few minutes later, locking the fuel tank up.

"You're the medic and the pilot. That means you're the one who has to make the decision. I'm nothing but your backup right now."

"I trust your instinct."

Shan didn't have a reply.

"I won't minimize how serious this is."

"I've seen people die from appendicitis, and I don't want to lose anyone else." She understood she wasn't responsible for the two officers that had been killed in January. This felt different.

"I can't guarantee anything right now, because he's sick and I have no way of helping him," he repeated.

"Have you ever done the surgery?"

"I've assisted a handful of times. With an actual doctor, in a hospital, and all the right equipment. Again, I have none of those." Green didn't sugar-coat it for her, knowing she could deal. "Honestly, we need to go now. I can't even be certain that's why he's sick."

"Then we're going now."

"You get the AKs, I'll get Chris."

This time, she didn't notice any motion sickness. Taking the seat next to Green, she kept a wary eye on Chris in the back. "Do we need to refuel at the state line?"

"It would be safer. If we're fighting a headwind all the way, we'll be low on reserves by the time we get to Lyons." They were already bouncing around, the space cramped, cold, and damp. "If this doesn't clear, we may get stuck on the ground there. The low pressure front should run north right along the mountains. Worse weather in Colorado than here."

"If this doesn't clear, we might need to turn back."

"I wasn't going to say it, not until I had to."

"Do I get any say in this?" Chris asked from the passenger's seat. His fever was steady.

"No," they both answered. The plane shook from the choppy air.

"I'm going to head east and climb, try to get ahead or above this," Green said, making sure she was aware of what he was doing. "Maybe," he repeated as they dropped suddenly and he struggled to level the plane out. After ten minutes of fighting turbulence, it was obvious the weather wasn't getting better. "We're burning a lot of fuel and I can't get decent altitude. If the conditions don't change, we'll have to have to detour farther east than I planned."

"What does that mean?" Shan asked.

"Hours of extra travel time. If we have to set down in an emergency, we could be a hundred miles from the refueling station."

"Where are we now?"

Green pulled up a map on the computer monitor. "We're the blinking red dot. Not much else works because there's no GPS."

"Yeah," she knew that, contemplating. "How far have we traveled?"

"About eighty miles east and north, but more east."

"That makes it about sixty miles to Angelfire."

Green didn't respond.

"Where in the hell is that?" Chris managed.

"Angelfire is the Caulder home base," Green said what Vance had told them. "A place not safe for all of us, especially those of us that are Gen En."

"It's not like they can tell what I am."

"Vance said they aren't allowed there. Did you ask him what they do if one wanders in?"

"I did, and he said they are asked to leave, politely, the first time.

They don't throw blind trust to Gen Ens, or anyone, and I don't blame them."

He couldn't tell if she was lying or not. "Capt. Allen, I can't take you there because of the potential risk."

"Yes, you can, Capt. Green. We have little choice."

"Would it do me any good to protest?"

She shook her head. "No. He needs to be in a hospital, and that's the closest one."

"I can't drop us in to a place that's openly hostile."

"I'm not going to tell them."

"Do you think it's a secret? Hunter and his brother know, and they're both Caulders." Touchy subject, and Green knew she was as likely to tell him to piss off as offer a civil answer. She didn't say a thing for several moments, and he was thinking she was going to pull rank on him. Command rank, if he had to guess.

"I understand your concerns, Damon. Program it in and take us to Angelfire. Let me deal with the rest, because I've been trained to deal with this. I know what I'm doing."

"This sort of thing? The sort of thing where people might want to kill you for no other reason than you're Gen En?"

"Rafe wanted to kill me for no other reason."

"That's my point."

"Politicians and sociopaths are different."

"You hope," he scoffed, only half joking.

"Take us to Angelfire. Don't tell them anything. Look after Chris. That's your job now. I release you from any oaths you swore to Wade before we ever ventured out into the world. I'll speak for us."

"Are you supposed to be out here, now? Is this some Command order?" He drew up a new flight plan and set it. "I don't want to hear the half-truths you tell the 'Conda."

"My assignment is to scout out potential allies in the south. Meaning south of Vance. Meaning Angelfire."

"That's why we've been edging closer for the past month."

"It is," she agreed. "This isn't how I'd planned on making contact.

Vance was going to do that for me. Diplomacy and all that, and out of the question now."

"Dammit, Shan, I don't like this. It's not even a plan."

"It's not up for debate."

"Don't make me have to rescue you later."

"I can't even respond to that," she frowned, imagining a lot of scenarios where that could happen.

"I get the last word this time."

Chapter Five

"We're clear," Green said, watching their progress on the computer. "Get on the radio and see if Angelfire is on the air." It was in the middle of the night, with a hell of a storm brewing up just to the south. His shoulders ached from fighting the wind and he had little confidence in the chances of anyone hearing them, but there was no safe alternative. Chris had been drifting in and out of consciousness for half an hour.

"Mayday, mayday, this is Cody Air One. Mayday, Angelfire airstrip, we have a medical emergency. Over," Shan announced, hoping the same thing he was, that there was someone out there to answer.

Static.

For an instant, he saw the same look in her eyes she'd had during the offensive in Manitou. Then it was gone, and she shook her head with determination. "Are you all right?" he asked, anyway.

"I will be when we get on the ground." Shan tried the radio again. "Mayday, mayday, please respond."

"What do we do in twenty minutes, when we get close to this supposed airfield?"

"Do we have enough fuel to make it to Lyons, straight-shot?"

He read the gauge and did some quick calculating. "It'll be close."

"I'll keep trying to raise someone on the radio. If there's a reply, problem solved. If not, we make for Estes Park. You find a road on your computer and hope twenty-year-old information is good. We get as close as we can, and call in an emergency at the Lyons airstrip."

"I'm glad you have that much confidence in my flying skills. My landing skills," Green corrected. "In deteriorating weather, the dark."

"I do," Shan said.

"You, Capt. Allen, are bat-shit crazy, then."

"Because I trust you?"

"Because you trust the mountains and the storm not to kill us tonight," he spoke in low tones, in case Chris was listening.

"Is that a Siksika thing?"

"It's a fear-of-dying thing."

"We've gotten ahead of the storm, and the mountains haven't killed us yet." About then, Chris started coughing and Shan moved back to a seat to check his vitals.

"Mayday, mayday, is anyone on this frequency?" Green tried his luck at it. "How's he doing?"

"Respiration is shallow. His fever is at 101.5, and he's still mostly unresponsive."

"We'll be passing the area of Angelfire soon. In thirty minutes, we won't be able to turn back," he said, double-checking his figures.

"Back to Angelfire, you mean?"

"We've been past going back to West Mesa since the minute we got off the ground," Green said. "By now, there's four or five inches of snow over a nice layer of ice."

Shan took a deep breath. "Try the radio."

"Mayday," he said dryly.

"Be serious." Shan moved back to the co-pilot's seat, taking the mic. "Mayday, Angelfire airstrip, please respond. This is Cody Air One. We have a medical emergency."

Green regarded her with skepticism.

"I swear someone is answering us."

"I'm not hearing it."

"I am. It's like filtering through water." She tried to sense it again.

Green took the mic. "Mayday, mayday."

"Can we head west?"

"From here, without a current topographical map? No, ma'am. I will not fly us into the side of a mountain."

The plane dropped abruptly from a downdraft and Shan braced herself on the dashboard, swearing, "Sonofabitch."

"Are you okay?" Green asked, aware Chris was strapped in better than they were.

"I don't like airplanes," she yelled.

"Cody Air One, this is Angelfire Airfield. What is your emergency?"

They looked at each other, both surprised. The signal was clear and close.

"Angelfire, this is a medical emergency," Shan answered, hoping a female voice would help sway their decision in her favor. "Possible ruptured appendix."

"Is the patient conscious?"

"No."

There was a long silence. "Standby."

"Cody Air One, please follow our instructions to the letter," an unfamiliar voice on the radio announced. "Our coordinates are N36°25.32' by W105°17.39'. Do you copy?"

"I got it," Green said, typing it in. The screen blinked, then updated. "Good to go. Tell them."

"We copy," Shan said.

"What are the specifications of your aircraft, over?"

She looked at Green, not having a clue. He took the handset. "Angelfire, this is a Cessna 210, standard model, over."

"How many passengers?"

"We are three."

"What is your point of origin?"

"Tell them, Cody," Shan instructed, thinking it was obvious.

"Cody."

"You are coming in from the south. Where did you depart from today?"

Shan resigned to the fact they were going to be grilled until whoever was sitting at the airport was satisfied with their answers. Vista Security would damned sure be certain before they let outsiders drop in on them. "Go ahead."

"Departed West Mesa just as a storm was setting in. I expect it will move in behind us soon," Green told them.

"Copy. When you touch down, follow the lights towards the hangars. Stop on the tarmac at Building A. It's marked in big, red letters. Do not exit your aircraft. A medical team will be waiting. We also have a tactical team that will clear you first. Are you carrying firearms, over?"

"Several."

"Do as you're instructed and we'll get this finished as quickly as possible. You're ten minutes from the landing strip. Over."

"Understood, over," Green answered. To Shan, he inquired, "You won't do anything unusual, will you?"

"No," she put on her best innocent face.

"Shannon, we need to figure this out now. You need to trust my instincts, too."

She groaned. "I do. First, we get Chris carted off to whatever hospital is closest. If this is the city, expect it to be twice the size of The Vista." The cloud cover was low. They hadn't been able to get a view of the valley.

Green blinked. He'd heard rumors. Having her confirm it was different.

"Speaking of The Vista, don't," she went on. "You know the protocol. As far as you're concerned, Cody is the center of the universe. Don't tell them anything other than your name. Refer all questions back to me. There's a chance they already know the basics."

"Caulder."

"Keep in mind, JT only knows what Vance and Hunter have told him, and Hunter is still Vista Security. He won't be saying much."

"Can we expect any help from the rest of Team Three?"

"No. Even if I could, I wouldn't. We need to make a good impression, one that says they can trust us. This is less than ideal circumstances to begin with, and you know how Wade can be."

"Has it occurred to you how inherently dangerous your orders are?" The plane started a long, easy turn to the west, Green flying rather than letting someone on the ground direct them by computer.

"Someone has to do this, and I volunteered. I'm a Scout."

"That doesn't mean you need to volunteer. I've already told you I don't agree with this."

"Protest noted. Stay with the rookie. I'll deal with Caulder or whatever minions he sends."

"What about Hunter?" Green asked. It was a dangerous, tricky, complicated question and he was sure it had been on her mind for the past few hours, at least a little.

Sitting back in her seat, Shan thought about it. "Are we losing altitude?" she evaded the question.

"On purpose, yes. We'll be able to see the runway lights any time now."

"I don't know about Hunter," she confessed.

"I have to ask. We're working as a team and that includes covering you, even if you're following orders. Even if you're not." He'd been part of the 'Conda too long not to recognize when they were wandering outside the boundaries set for them.

"Ask me anything else."

"Other than getting to Angelfire, do you have any orders?" While Wade thrived on making plans, Shan scorned the idea.

"This unscheduled stop has made everything void." She waved her hand in disgust, knowing the next question. "Yes, it's an accident that we're going to where Hunter is. If I'd wanted to go with him, I'd have done it weeks ago when he left Estes Park. I had other things I was supposed to do before finding my way to Angelfire."

"I don't suppose you'd care to tell me what the team was working on?"

"We were trying to decide which of us would be the safest one to go speak with their council."

"Meaning you and Wade were arguing over who went in first."

"No. All of us had an interest. We're attempting to find potential allies, and I got Angelfire for obvious reasons. It's not an absolute that the three of us can't go out in the world like we've always planned."

"As a team?"

"Together, yes, not as a team. As people."

"Runway lights," Green said, correcting their course. He shouldn't have been surprised by the idea, but it caught him off-guard. "We'll be on the ground in two minutes."

"I'm going to talk to Chris. Do what they tell you."

The plane bounced along a rough runway that smoothed out as they neared the hangars. Several vehicles sat outside and by the time they stopped in front of the designated building, a group of people had emerged. They wore military-style gear, the heavy winter type, and were as well-armed as Vista Security.

It took a few minutes to have all their weaponry confiscated, Shan and Green passing them to the masked guards, who targeted them the entire time. Then they were ordered out, Shan first, hands up. Two grabbed her and led her into the hangar. Green followed a few seconds later as an ambulance pulled up.

"I'm Major Walden," a tall, balding man of fifty-something announced, approaching them. He wore camos, crisp and pressed, a heavy parka, shined boots, and a .45 on his hip. "Who's in charge of this ... little expedition?" He was no-nonsense and condescending enough to annoy both Vistans. It was a ploy.

"I am," Shan answered. "Capt. Allen." They watched Chris get loaded into the ambulance. "I'd like to request we accompany him to your facility."

"I've been instructed to detain you."

"Detain me. Let him," she indicated Green, "go to the hospital.

He's our pilot and our medic. I'm in charge of the scouting expedition."

Walden seemed skeptical. Green was muscular, as tall as the Major, and carrying a bit of an attitude. "Captain Allen," he said, trying to decide how seriously he was going to take her. "Captain of what?"

"Send Capt. Green to the hospital with Officer Taylor and we can talk about it for the rest of the night."

"You understand, she's taking responsibility for your actions while you're in Angelfire," Walden told Green, after considering her words for a long minute.

"I know," Green said.

Shannon was certain Green wanted to punch Walden in the face.

"Go," Walden dismissed, nodding for the guards to let him pass. "We'll be at the detention office until we figure out what to do with our unexpected guests." He opened the back door of an SUV. "You understand our caution, Capt. Allen."

"I do," she agreed, climbing in. It was four-wheel drive, black, roll cage, prisoner partition, tinted windows, and a well-armed driver. For a moment, she considered how much she could like this place. "Four speed or five speed?" she asked, getting comfortable.

"Five speed," he said. "You promised to answer my questions, and I'll be passing those answers along. Why were you at West Mesa?" he asked, not waiting to get to the jail.

"There's an airstrip."

"I'm aware. How did you find out about it?"

Shan decided to name-drop. It might keep her out of lock-up for the rest of the night, but she was doubtful. Walden was following orders. It was what he did. "Up at Estes Park, Councilor Vance gave us maps to a handful of airstrips."

"Vance doesn't hand that information out to just anyone."

"We've been doing some scouting missions nearby for the past few months. This one was, admittedly, a bit of a risk. Not the sort of problem we expected, or could deal with on our own," she shrugged. The drive was across the street. They pulled into an empty lot and since the one story building didn't have windows, she figured they were at the jail. It started snowing, huge, wet flakes, as they parked.

The driver opened the door, as there was no handle on the inside. He let her walk in on her own, Walden right beside her. It was a jail, complete with barred windows and doors that had to be opened by a guard on the other side. Shan started thinking it might have been smarter to let Green take her place and go to the hospital with Chris.

"Sit," Walden directed, pointing at a chair in the first office as he spoke with the duty officer. She did, leaning forward so she could look down the hall. "There's nothing interesting out there," he said, a few moments later, taking the seat behind the desk and pushing back. "I assume you've seen a detention facility before. In Cody perhaps."

"I've seen a jail before."

"You were going to tell me all about yourself," he reminded her. "Who are you affiliated with?"

"Cody Security. We're a Scout team."

"And you're the senior officer," he repeated. "Is your chain-of-command based on the military or civilian police?"

"A little of each."

"How many officers are there in Cody? How many civilians?"

"I can't tell you that," Shan said. "Ask me something I can answer."

"Give me a good reason I shouldn't put you in a cell until I figure out what to do with you," he challenged.

Part of his problem with her was the fact that she was female and young. Shan had that figured out a few moments after they met. "I'm no threat to you or anyone else here. If we didn't have an emergency, you wouldn't have known about us until Vance got permission to send us here."

He sighed. "If we hadn't received reports about you earlier this year, we wouldn't have let you land. That doesn't change the fact you're outsiders. Vance vouching for you doesn't change it. Out of an abundance of caution, and decades of hindsight, I'm locking you safely away for the night. That way, your teammates will behave, you'll be staying put, and all the questions we have can be dealt with in the morning, when the people who have a little more insight into your situation will be here."

"What people?"

"Like you, I'm not at liberty to discuss our policies and procedures." He stood. "I recommend getting some sleep. The cells are secure, but you're in isolation here until I'm told you're not. Is there anything you require?"

"I'd like an update on my officers. Other than that, no."

The cell was a twelve by twelve foot standard holding cell, with a concrete partition dividing off a toilet and sink, a single bunk with bedding, recessed lighting in the ceiling. Bottled water and some sort of rations pack all in plastic. The lock on the door was magnetic rather than keyed, not that she had any plans for a jailbreak. They'd walked through what she assumed were two metal detectors on the way to the wing.

"If you need something, call out. An officer is monitoring the floor from the Communications Center. Otherwise, expect breakfast at 6am. I'm uncertain when an OIC will be in with the weather turning." Walden was polite, professional, and starched. "The lights will go out in fifteen minutes. Good night, Capt. Allen." Then he closed the door.

Wondering what he'd been told in those few moments after their arrival, Shan kicked off her boots and tried to rest. She'd never realized she was claustrophobic.

Chapter Six

Cody noon April 8

"There are seven of them, sitting at the edge of the frontage road, next ridge east," Ballentyne reported, peering through binoculars. The roof of the station was an unlikely place for a shift debriefing, but there they were, watching the intruders edge closer and closer. It was almost a daily event. "They want us to see them. Four are wearing winter camos, two in forest camos, one is wearing blue jeans and a military green flak jacket. All of them are armed, faces covered. I can only guess they're male. Military or not, again, a guess."

"They know we're here, and that we're watching them," Mac said, bringing his own pair of binoculars to use. "It looks like the same band. Being able to sneak in this close, and not approaching any of our two-man teams, is a concern. If they want to hurt us, they could."

"What are you going to do?" Ballentyne asked.

"How long have they been there?"

"Over an hour now."

"I'm going to get a horse, ride over there, and invite them back for lunch. It seems like a good idea."

"Lambert will have a heart attack."

Mac shrugged, unconcerned. "He'll quote regulations, sure. And then what? I'm in command of the base."

"Exactly why he'll say you can't go out there."

"And exactly why I am."

"Alone?"

"You can come with me." Mac glanced sideways, knowing he would.

"They're baiting us, daring us to go out there," Ballentyne said, peering at Mac for a moment.

"You're the one always reminding me, not everything happens with ill-intent."

"I've never said 'ill-intent' in my life."

"Me either, until just now. You know what I mean. We're here to find other people. So we go introduce ourselves to these other people and see what happens."

"Fine. Let's go now, before Lambert hears. If we both get killed, he inherits the base."

Mac didn't think that was quite so funny. "He'd hate that."

"And bribe my partner into taking the job."

"Truth."

The plan worked well until they made it to the lobby. Lambert was coming in the main door as they emerged from the stairwell. "You've seen them," he greeted, ready to call an alert.

"Yes," Mac said. "We're going to take care of it."

"How so?"

"You're in charge until I get back," Mac continued. "I don't see the point of a lock-down. When we do that, they just fade in to the forest and come back the next day. I'm going to go find out why."

Lambert considered arguing, then he considered how successful that tactic had been in the past. "At least let me send a patrol with you."

Ballentyne agreed, "That's not a bad idea. Four of us, someone can stand on the roof and keep an eye out. A sniper would be best."

"We could follow them halfway to Kansas," Mac said. "Call a patrol to the plaza. We're gone as soon as they get here."

"Halfway to South Dakota," Lambert corrected. "There's a city in South Dakota, across the dotted line. We could make a week of it. A month, if we want to be realistic." All three grinned. The dotted lines, the old state boundaries, meant little anymore.

"If they ride back in here with us, do nothing other than call in an extra team and a general alert. These people already know our routine. Let's introduce ourselves and make some allies."

"You don't think they have any nefarious plans?"

"I don't. I'm going to confirm it, one way or the other. Stay sharp, get everyone moving."

"If you make me have to radio Shannon and tell her you got killed because you were stupid, it's going to ruin everyone's day." It was Lambert's way of telling them to be careful.

"Me, or him?" Ballentyne asked, pretending to be insulted.

"Both of you," Lambert said. "What's the timetable?"

Mac raised his eyebrows, speculating. He hadn't considered it yet. "Wait until morning to worry, if we're not back by dark."

"I need a serious answer."

"We'll call in within the hour. Follow protocol if we don't."

"Send out twenty people with guns," Lambert said, offhanded. "In the morning."

"If we want to make ourselves any more obvious," Ballentyne observed, riding next to Mac, with two officers behind them. "We can break out a bullhorn." Keeping to the center of the road, they didn't conceal their weapons, but they weren't locked and loaded, either.

"They'll show up when they want, or disappear back into the mountains," Mac said.

"Or show up when they want to," he repeated, seeing riders emerging on the street in the cul-de-sac a quarter mile ahead.

"We're here to talk, not shoot the neighbors," Mac reminded them. "And I get to do the talking. Stay sharp, and stay here."

"I'm going with you," Ballentyne said.

"I was aware," Mac said. Two riders broke off from the group and came towards them.

"Nice day for a ride," one of the pair greeted, unwrapping the scarf from around his face. "Early for it, but no complaints."

"It is," Mac agreed. They'd all stopped about twenty feet apart, close enough to make it personal. It was nice, too; clear skies, with the scent of pine and sage on the breeze. "You've been out here for a few nice days. What were you going to do if it snowed?"

"We have a camp, close," he indicated somewhere vaguely to the east.

Mac could sense Ballentyne's level of tension ratchet up a notch.

"We weren't aware of that, but it makes sense," Mac admitted. "There were two surveys of the area over the past few years. You must camouflage well."

"I hope so," the rider chuckled. "That's the intent, not to be discovered, unless we want to be. Like now."

"Are we intruding on your property?" Mac asked, a straightforward approach seeming the best bet.

"Cody? No. We're a little more off the beaten path. Fewer intrusions, easier to defend. I think you know what I mean." He was in his forties, sandy-haired, well-armed, and not in a hurry to give away too much.

"I have an idea," Mac said. "We're setting up a permanent place. We're not here to make enemies."

"It's been interesting, watching all the activity after so long. Where did you migrate in from?"

"Up north." Mac could be just as vague.

"Like we're 'out east'," the rider smiled, maneuvering his horse closer, extending his hand. "I'm Harlan."

"Mac." They shook hands, taking stock of each other.

"We've been hearing some talk about a new clan running roughshod through the Front Range this past year. I can confirm some of those rumors myself. A week ago, I got an interesting video of a stronghold in central Colorado."

"A stronghold? Of what sort?" Mac asked, meaning to sound oblivious.

"Not one of the havens. This was far from a safe zone. Point being, it's not there now. Someone bombed it out of existence. It was a relief to the havens in the area. I don't suppose you'd heard anything?"

"There's been little contact outside Cody, recently. We all have exploits to brag about. If you feel safe, we should go settle in, get a warm meal, and discuss why we're here and why you care."

"Invitation accepted," Harlan decided. "You're going to let us ride in to a camp you've barely had time to organize?"

"We're a bit organized," Mac admitted. "We're more than seven, and we've been watching you, too."

"Outstanding."

"You're going to ride in to a place you know nothing about, on the word of a stranger?"

"If you were a danger to us, you'd never have been aware we were here," Harlan said.

"Good point. Remember to tell me more about this new clan, the havens, and these safe-zones."

"Oh, I'll remember," Harlan said. "You can tell me more about 'up north'. I haven't been past Wyoming in two decades. Used to be some good hunting, up in Montana."

Mac nodded, understanding Harlan was more aware of current events than what he let on. The day finally showed some promise. "It's a deal."

The gunshots sounded close, cracking in the morning air, sharp and clear. One, two, three, echoing across the valley, then silence. Wade was off his horse, gun drawn, against a tree trunk for cover a split second after the first report. He stayed there, barely breathing, and waited. There would be more fire in response, or something human and far more wrenching.

The shouting was muffled and distant enough that he couldn't determine what was going. He reached, searching for the sensations happening out of his line-of-sight, perhaps a half of a mile away.

Fear was the predominant impression he sensed. Several travelers, male and female, moving away, flight rather than fight. The aggressors hesitated, uncertain where their prey was. Wade imagined it wasn't the first time the two groups had clashed. There seemed to be more than a casual recognition.

He returned to his horse and unstrapped the long gun, pulling ammo packs for the .45 out and pocketing them, no intention of becoming a victim. He intended to get a first-hand account of what was happening right up the long-abandoned highway. Far from the first encounter with other people that his ever-widening search pattern had produced, the difference this time was circumstances. They weren't his people or his responsibility, but it would be a cold day in hell when he let the defenseless die and didn't try to put a stop to it.

They had scattered. From the tracks in the thin layer of mud, he could see several people were moving away from the road, running. Horses as well. Wade slung his sniper rifle over his shoulder, making his way into the trees on the far side. From here, the valley dipped sharply, and the forest broke into fields. Another fifty or sixty miles east, the mountains fell away to the Great Plains. He wouldn't be going east because of the many red zones. Heavy underbrush forced him back onto the road after a short distance. It didn't take long for him to attract attention, out in the open.

"Hey," a male voice demanded attention, coming up behind him. "What do you think you're doing?"

Dropping the reins, Wade turned towards him. Seeing two on the road and a third on the shoulder, he drew his sidearm as he strode towards them. In forest camos and packing a lot of tactical gear, he was intimidating. "I'm walking because my horse is tired. What are you doing?" he emphasized, keeping the weapon obvious in hand.

"Looking for someone," the other quickly said. "Not you."

"Drop your gun," the one standing in the weeds shouted, pointing a small caliber rifle at him.

"That's not happening," Wade told them, stopping.

"He's not one of them," the second man repeated. "We'll be moving along."

"Were you shooting at the people you're looking for?" Wade asked, not stepping aside for them.

"They shot at us, earlier. It's not your concern," the first said.

He wasn't lying, at least the part about being shot at. Wade put them right in the same category as any Scavenger that he'd ever crossed paths with. He moved out of the way. "I didn't start the conversation." They kept wary eyes on each other until they rounded a curve in the road and were out of sight.

Wade mounted up and cut to the game trail he'd found along the other side of the road. He didn't trust that they wouldn't come looking for him later, and he didn't believe they were the innocent victims of some imagined crime. It would be dark soon. He worked better in the night.

The moon in the last quarter, and even the shadows were muted. Donning the rest of his gear, Wade left the horse and followed not-so-subtle voices. The three had caught up with a group of travelers, two men, two women and four children not yet teenagers. The youngest were sitting on the ground, crying, while the three Scavengers went about threatening them.

Tossing a smoke grenade near the center of the group diffused the imminent threat, if only for a moment, and Wade came in to the light, firing. Two down and the third returned fire. He wanted to leave one alive to question, but the chance of civilians getting injured ratcheted up fast. A snap decision, he took down the third, never flinching or wavering.

One man grabbed a dropped pistol and Wade swung around to take aim at him. "If I was here to kill you, you'd already be dead," he said, muffled and distorted through the mask, indicating those already dead. "Drop it."

He did. "There are more of them, a lot more of them, and they heard that."

"The reason all of you are packing up and moving now," Wade said, pulling the gas mask off.

"In the dark?" one of the women asked.

"Unless you want to wait around here for a few more hours and see what daylight brings," Wade told her. "How many more are there?"

"After we left Alma, there were close to twenty of them. This last day, only six or seven," the other surviving man offered.

"Twenty?" Wade repeated. "What did you do to attract that kind of attention?"

"We left the village. They told us in the fall it would be better to wait until spring. Last week, when the weather broke, they told us it would be better to wait until the middle of summer."

Wade nodded. "So you packed as much as you could carry and ran off in the middle of the night?"

"Yes," the woman said. "They told us we had to have permission to leave. We had to have permission to do anything."

"How long had you lived there?"

"We got there in August, just before the snow."

"Did you have a plan on where to go?" Wade grilled them. "Or did you think you would wander in the mountains and survive off the land?" The children had stopped crying, at least.

"There are safe havens all across the mountains. We're trying to find one."

Wade shook his head. "There are radiation fields and Scavengers, too. Follow the road west. South is too far."

"Have you been to them, the havens?" another of the men ventured.

"The one in Estes Park. It's too far to drag those kids. Plus, there are two of those radiation fields on the way. Unless you have an accurate map, it's too dangerous. How much did you steal from them?"

"We had our own supplies, and they took everything. When we left, we took what was fair."

"Do you have a map?" They did, and they peered at it by the light of the fading campfire. "Here," he pointed out. "Go here. Head west, don't stop until dark tomorrow night. Their horses are hobbled in the gully just to the east."

"What if they follow us?" the woman asked, gathering the kids.

"I'm waiting close by for a few hours. If they come through here, they won't be following you or anyone, ever again."

"Why are you helping us?"

"I ask myself that, all the time," Wade said, knowing there was no other way he could live, not really.

Daybreak, and the best Shan had managed, was dozing for a few minutes at a time. She'd been restless, pacing for a time before trying to sleep. A book would have occupied her, but she hadn't thought to ask for one.

"Capt. Allen?" a male voice on the intercom inquired. "I assume you're awake."

"Yes, I am." She sat up, wondering how ragged she looked, feeling worse from the long flight and lockup. Neither were things she wanted to do again.

"I'm supposed to relay to you that Officer Taylor came out of surgery fine and was resting well at the hospital. Officer Green is with him, at your request."

"Thank you. Has an OIC been contacted about us yet?"

"Last night, before you landed. The weather has been making travel difficult. Someone will be in soon to see you."

True to his word, a few minutes later, she listened to the door at the end of the hall open. Shan hoped her first impression hadn't been as crude or desperate as she remembered it.

"You can stay there and wait for the Day Officer," the dark-haired man dressed as a civilian, in blue jeans and a black thermal shirt offered, using a key-card to open the door. Tall, well-built and maybe in his late twenties. He wore no visible weapons. "Or we can go to the mess hall and have a private conversation."

Shan was skeptical. She wondered if he'd been taller than Hunter, the last time they'd been together, before the war. Unlikely, she decided, as he'd been six years old and Hunter, ten. He was the taller one now.

"What were you just thinking?" he asked.

"Was your brother surprised you don't have to look up at him now?"

He broke into a smile. "I'm JT, and I take after our father. Hunter favors our mother. We had two decades worth of catching up. I'm sure he noticed."

"I'd like to go to the hospital and see my officers."

"In time," he said. "We need to talk first."

Every word they spoke was going to be scrutinized by each of them. Shan listened, looking up at the closest camera.

"I turned them off when I came in," he said. "Across the street is less intrusive. We'll go to the hospital later. You can talk to your people, get a change of clothes and a shower if you'd like."

"I've been told you have an aversion to certain clans. Ones I may or may not be associated with. I'd like to see where I stand."

He moved into the cell a few steps and spoke in a low tone. "My brother assures me I have no reason not to trust you. The concerns about these other clans are things best discussed later."

"Oh, we will. Is this all legal and such? I'd rather not get on anyone's bad side on my first day here."

"It is," JT said. "I've signed you out, and vouched for your good behavior."

Shan followed him out, taking careful stock of the facility. They stopped in the foyer and she picked up her parka from a box of her belongings. Her handguns and knives weren't included. Once outside, she had a view of how bad the storm had been, with over a foot of snow on the ground. The night before, it had been a dusting. The entire landscape was painted in a layer of ice and snow that hadn't begun melting yet. "What's the elevation here?" she asked, the air thin and bitter cold.

"Nine thousand feet," JT said. "It depends where you're at in the valley. Is that why you're here, for a topographical survey?"

"I'm here because we had no other choice. You don't think we faked a medical emergency to sneak in here when Vance was going to send us in a few weeks, anyway?"

"No one thinks that. They have to wonder why you were spying on us."

"We weren't spying on you," she scoffed. "That's making your haven a little more important to us than it is."

He held the door for her. The mess hall was a pleasant-looking diner between the jail and what she assumed was a barracks of some sort. They found a booth in the back, having their choice as they were the first customers.

"Is this conversation between you and I, or is it going to be shared with any of the Councilors?" she asked. "Including your father."

"This is between you and me. The point is, I know all about you, Capt. Allen. I've known for years, when we didn't have names and faces to go with the stories."

"Before we got to Estes Park, you wanted Vance to figure out a way of stopping us."

"I perceived you as a threat to the stability of the area. After January, I can't think I was wrong."

"What happened in January?"

"I could ask you the same thing." Seeing she wasn't going to answer, he waited for the attendant to leave trays of food before answering. "Vance said Rafe was no longer our problem. He seldom gives me details on his issues, and this was no different."

"You assumed we had a hand in Rafe no longer being a problem. Did you ask Hunter?"

"Are you reading me?"

"Not in the way Rafe could, no. I don't have that ability."

"Would you be able to tell the truth from a lie?"

"It depends on a lot of variables. I'm taking your word as the truth because we have no reason to lie to each other. You already are aware of what I am, and I understand the implications of that."

"No, I didn't ask him. He has loyalties to The Vista, and those choices are his. You've met Rafe, though," JT pursued the idea.

"I've crossed paths with him."

"Under what circumstances?"

"The reason any of us are here and in Colorado. Last July, he shot my partner and I in an ambush near The Vista. Later, he told me Wade was his target."

"Where is Wade now?"

"Colorado."

"That's the same thing Vance said. The problem, I don't believe you," JT told her. "It's a simple thing, but I don't."

"I understand your caution," she said, looking for neutral ground. Her meal included eggs, hash brown potatoes with mushrooms, onions, and peppers, bacon and sausage, a glass of milk and another glass of something she couldn't identify. Shan sniffed it.

"It's orange juice."

"What does it taste like?"

"Oranges. Citrus fruit. Vitamin C keeps people from getting scurvy. What does The Vista harvest?" he made conversation.

"Kale, onions, potatoes, strawberries. Things that are a lot easier to grow than citrus fruit."

"We don't have a lot of them, but you are a guest. Some people even like it."

Shan tasted it, deciding it wouldn't kill her to appease him. "Not bad."

"It doesn't hurt to develop new tastes."

"I don't blame you for not trusting us," Shan said. "I don't think Wade will ever have trust again. We've been alone all our lives, trying to figure out why we were different and afraid to tell anyone."

JT considered it. Young Altered, young children, with no clue, suddenly alone and on their own in a world at war with itself. "What are your immediate goals?"

"To establish contact with other places, and learn what's happened in the past twenty years. I can imagine The Vista will want to become a haven."

"That will take time."

"It's not so simple on our side, either. Cody has different goals. We don't have to be in line with your havens. We aren't here for you. The safety of The Vista is first."

"When you say 'we', who do you mean?"

It was her turn to consider an answer. "I can speak for Team Three and the 'Conda right now. That's Wade's private security group and they're in charge of Cody."

"Vance sent me south to avoid meeting Team Three right off. Those trust issues again. The least we can do is to be honest with each other."

"I am. There are things I'm unaware of."

"Fine. This is easy. You met with a faction of The Sixth in December."

"We've already told Vance what we knew."

JT shook his head, not satisfied with the answer. "I need to hear your version, not his. Vance doesn't share most information with me or with Angelfire."

"Who are you representing?" Shan asked. If he said Vance, the conversation was over.

"I'm here out of my curiosity, and because Councilor Caulder asked me to assess the situation for him. I advised him to not let his military officers question you."

"Not anyone affiliated with Estes Park?"

"No. Why?"

"I've been advised we are not allies."

"As much as my father has set himself apart from The Altered, I've learned what I can about them. You, The Vista, Cody, all of you, could be an asset to us as allies. There are many ways we can help reach other. I understood letting Walden use intimidation would get nothing from you."

"You're right–we're not your enemy," Shan said.

"Yet you hide yourself in your own home."

She had to give JT that. "He called himself Kaden. There was a lot of small talk and he didn't tell us anything I couldn't have figured out. We got sent back to Estes Park the next morning." Shan saw it as the truth, at least from her perspective. It was what Hunter would say happened. JT had asked.

"What did he tell you, about you?"

"He said there might have been millions of us before the war, but no records survived, no way to know. He explained how the Gen En, The Altered, were raised and trained, before." Shan picked at her food, enjoying the vegetables.

"Did he tell you what synthesis you were?"

"Synthesis," she repeated.

"What do you call it?"

"Generations. We are aware it's incorrect."

"It was an amalgam, a blend of many processes. A generation, if you will, is a misnomer, but one that various entities used."

"I honestly didn't want to hear about it," Shan told him.

Puzzled, he wondered what her ploy was. "The Altered are curious. Some of you are brilliant. Most of you are more intelligent than you let others see. You soak up new information."

Cutting him off, Shan kept her voice low, level. "We figured out what we might be from old media information that survived. Wade pieced it together when he was ten. No one, no one, offered us any advice or help and he made sure we kept ourselves hidden. Those same media stories said people hated us and feared us and didn't think we should be allowed to live. When I say I don't want to know about what came before, I'm not being flippant."

"You're hiding from the past, from what you are."

"Do you blame me? We're trying to do better. We've kept to The Vista too long and stepped into the middle of another war. That's not what we want, but you saw what happened in Manitou. That was self-defense. Do you know what Rafe did, twelve years ago?"

"Rumors. Vance wouldn't elaborate."

"Vance was there," Shan said, shivering from the image in the back of her mind. The mushroom cloud to the east, burning in the evening sky. "He said Rafe launched the ICBM, and he detonated it seconds later."

"Has it occurred to you that Vance might have lied?"

"Every moment of the day. Why would Rafe go to the trouble of launching a dead missile, then detonate it before it reached a target?"

"Did you and Wade see it?"

Shannon blinked.

"Vance is an early synthesis," JT pointed out the error in her thinking. "Oh, he's trained and dangerous, make no mistake. He doesn't have the ability to do what he claims, and by that, I mean detonate the warhead."

"Rafe did." The realization surprised her. Of all the scenarios she'd played in her mind, that he'd done it to find them wasn't one. To her, it had always been an accident.

"Over time, we've gotten several versions of the events from people involved. Altered and not. Rafe set off the ICBM on The Vista's doorstep to see if there was a response. An Altered response."

"And there was." She took a deep breath, wondering if she could send Green to evac the Vistans. Any idea of his true motives scared her. She wanted the team out of Estes Park. "Two of us."

"No, Capt. Allen, dozens. The only ones he had an interest in were the pair that recognized their abilities. So, did Kaden tell you what generation you are?" He finished eating, far more interested in what she had to say.

"He said, the fourteenth."

"Do you know what that means?"

"A joke. The thirteenth, but the people in charge wouldn't call it that because of some inane superstition."

JT realized how right Vance had been, way back before they made it to Estes Park. The Vistans were too damned smart for their own good. Well-trained, too. She wasn't telling him anything of significance, either. Plus, they'd set Rafe up in his own home, with no help from Vance. Allies to make or break a haven or be the final wedge between Angelfire and Estes Park. It was his job to make sure that the latter didn't happen.

"The fourteenth are a simple offshoot of The Sixth."

"You learn something new every day," Shan wrinkled her nose, undecided if it was accurate. It might be, but she didn't have all the facts to decide. "Is Councilor Caulder going to allow us in the city?"

"You'll have to ask him. Your status, as far as everyone else in Angelfire is concerned, is that you're a Cody Security officer doing recon. At the request of my brother, and because you're responsible for my family being whole again, I've kept certain information to myself. Make your case to the Councilor. If he ever questions you about being Altered, I'd suggest you not lie to him. I'll deny ever knowing it."

"Understood. Can I see Hunter?"

"He's not in the city right now, and when we can contact him, we will. For now, let's go visit your officers." JT had been expecting the question sooner.

"I'm still responsible for him, for your brother. Did he tell you that?"

JT nodded, "He said you'd mention it." More to that conversation as well, things he'd not discuss with her, things between brothers.

Despite his aversion to The Altered, he couldn't fault her for that. He might even like her. "I'm responsible for you right now. Don't make me regret the decision later."

Chapter Seven

Cody evening shift change April 11

"Not bad for a few months of work," Harlan said, watching from the balcony of the former dormitory dubbed Pod One. Security used it as a lookout, but most mornings, Mac had breakfast there, enjoying the sunrise. This evening, they were waiting for word from Harlan's riders and a Cody scout team investigating fires they'd spotted earlier out to the southeast.

"I'd like to take credit for all this, but honestly, plans for this happened before I was old enough to care," Mac admitted. "The buildings on the quad had to have been built just prior the war. Minor weather damage. Utilities were online inside a month."

"I meant you've organized, you've set priorities."

"A lot of people were involved in getting Cody up and running. Some of them are here, but most of them aren't. We're just the soldiers keeping watch."

"I'd like to see The Vista," Harlan said. "I have ulterior motives in offering our help."

"That's not a problem. I have ulterior motives in showing you what we're doing. We'll want to be included in at least the trade routes. Use Cody as the gateway for goods moving both directions. When we get that far, of course. What I'm not sure of is where to start."

Harlan thought about it. "Black Hills isn't a haven, and for more than one reason. Some of those are going to be the same reasons that cause you problems."

"I don't know what to expect. Your insight is a valuable commodity." It wasn't difficult for Mac to see him as former military. Harlan was disciplined, right-to-the-point, and far more cautious than he pretended to be.

"It's early, only three months on, but rumors don't take long to spread like wildfire. Even if you didn't wreck the stronghold, people will question if you had a part of it. Cody suddenly appears and someone takes out Manitou. The Board of Councilors, the Angelfire Assembly, will consider every scenario, and they'll make it hell for you to become a haven if they decide to. The same questions, time after time, while they look for a mistake in your story."

"This stronghold wasn't a haven, it was a base of operations for a gang of marauders."

Harlan nodded. "Close enough. Outlaws, raiders, call them what you want. They were dug in for a good decade, and no one had been able to deal with them."

"The Board is going to hold it against us, that we might have put an end to a band of outlaws? I'd want to thank them rather than punish them. Whoever drove them out," he said, not quite ready to confess.

"This particular band of outlaws was led by a particularly difficult Altered who set himself up there and was strangling the trade routes nearby," Harlan explained. "They've been waiting for someone to break the hold, drive them out as you said."

"Someone did. Again, they'd hold this against us for what reason?"

"They'll consider the people who killed him were Altered as well. Knowing Rafe and the defenses he had, I'd agree with them."

Alarms went off in Mac's thoughts. One of Rafe's scorned partners. "If we had The Altered here, what would that mean?"

"Certain board members won't tolerate the Altered in their city. A definite prejudice exists, and Rafe's at least partially responsible. The Board leaves governing up to each haven, as long as the basic tenets are upheld."

"Those tenets being?"

"To protect the populace, to provide shelter to those in need and to improve and advance the holdings of the havens through trade and other means."

"Sounds simple enough," Mac said, not serious. They both laughed. "The Vista qualifies. I couldn't tell you if there are Altered."

"I wouldn't expect you to. We're both smart enough to understand that. Again, there will be questions, ones you'll answer, or be like us, and stuck in the limbo of hoping to be being a haven, someday."

"We've been in limbo in The Vista for twenty years," Mac said. "If we hadn't forced the move to Cody, we'd still be isolated."

Harlan contemplated the things they'd discussed over the past days. He didn't expect to be Mac's new best friend, but they'd been straightforward with each other at least. "Did you, or others from The Vista go into Manitou in January and obliterated the stronghold?"

"I'm not at liberty to discuss our operations."

"You're in command here. It's your decision."

"True, but there are people I answer to, just like you," Mac said, suspecting there was far more to his story. Harlan could be the key to finding out who controlled the Front Range. "It is my decision."

"'Forced the move' out of The Vista. Why? Did The Altered shun you, or are you the shunned Altered?"

"I'm not ..." Mac began.

"At liberty to discuss," Harlan finished. "So, what are you at liberty to discuss, Commander? You said the decisions here are yours." He pushed back in his seat, awaiting an answer.

"I'm aware of what happened in January," Mac answered after contemplating where the conversation would go next.

"One question I want you to be honest about. Between you and me and no one else, because it's that important. Did someone kill Rafe?"

"I can't divulge details."

"My reasons are personal."

Mac sighed. So were his. "He didn't get away."

Harlan looked relieved. "After we've known each other a few years, I might explain the significance of that."

"I have an idea."

"An idea. Whatever he did, what he might have told you, other things he's done were far worse."

"I believe you," Mac said.

"To confirm you were in Manitou, tell me something to prove it." Harlan hadn't survived by being careless.

"I didn't say I was there. I said I was aware of what happened."

"And I said this was between you and me."

"If you'd been observing him, you know what was at the north end, at the top of the plateau."

"Go on," Harlan nodded.

"We have two well-maintained Cessnas. I can take you over to the hangar in the morning and show them to you."

"Just two?"

"There wasn't a third pilot available."

"I won't ask how you got those planes."

"Details. I can't divulge them. Let's say I have contact with certain people who know other people, out here in the world."

"Good enough answer. These scattered groups bothering you now will give up and move on, as long as they see you're persistent and well-armed."

"That we are," Mac said. "The fires," he went with the change of the subject, looking out eastward. "They're not accidental. Do you have problems with raiders in Black Hills?"

"Occasionally. Less in the past four or five years. Word gets around which cities are protected."

"They've been annoying us since we set up. They scatter the game, block a road we've been using, set fires, little things. We figured they're testing us. We thought you were them, at first. How do we get in contact with whoever we need to rejoin civilization? Such as it is."

"You don't. You let them. I wouldn't think you'll have to wait long. Don't get impatient. Everything they do is a test. Remember that and you might be a haven before we are. Also be aware, they can blacklist you and then you're in for years of trying to conform to their standards. If that's something you want."

"How do you get blacklisted?" Mac asked.

"The Altered, of course. Laws that conflict with theirs. That could be anything from capital punishment to fair trade. They use the threat."

"They did it to you, to Black Hills."

"Before my time. I'm cleaning up all the things left behind. Being self-sufficient isn't as easy as it sounds."

"The Vista has been, all this time. We don't need the trade routes to survive. We want to expand."

Harlan nodded. "That's where you need to be careful. The Vista is important because of that, because you've survived in isolation. Be cautious of who you call allies."

Mac understood it was a warning. It didn't need to be subtle. "Why are they holding up your status as a haven?"

"You tell me about your Altered and I'll tell you all about Black Hills. Hell, I'll tell you about Estes Park, Manitou, and all the places in between," Harlan mused.

Mac smiled. "If I told you, I'd have to kill you." He was only a little serious.

"Do you want to be a haven, or do you want to be in charge of your own life?" Harlan asked.

"What's your point?"

"Between The Vista, Cody, and Black Hills, we could do this. We could start our own routes, without their rules, and without their interference. It won't be easy, it won't be quick, and there will be resistance from the havens. Vocal resistance, for the most part. It's something we need to consider."

"I agree," Mac said. First with his officers, then Command. If this panned out, it would be bigger than anything they'd imagined. "How are we going to figure out a way to trust each other?"

Wade got to the edge of the village towards midday and stopped for a few minutes to stow his tactical gear. He wanted to appear as innocuous as possible. The people he'd been shadowing the past hundred miles had come in hours earlier, ragged and exhausted, but alive. Those kids would be safe here, or at least safer than traveling.

The road twisted around, following the river, turning from paved to dirt where the canyon narrowed. Easy defense, he decided, waiting for the gang of armed men to come off the hillside and confront him. He'd spotted them miles back. They came down after a few minutes, not as skittish as he thought they'd be. The smaller villages were easy targets, but then, this one had the advantage of being a haven. Hidden defenses, perhaps. It was how he'd set it up.

"Drop your weapons," one of them yelled across the hundred yards between them, long gun in hand.

Wade dismounted, moving slowly and with a purpose. He placed the .45 on the ground and backed away. Holding up his hands, he waited for further instructions.

"The saddle gun, too."

Using one hand and leaving the other up and visible, he tugged the shotgun free and put it down. "Your move," he called. There were four more firearms in his gear they couldn't see.

"Stand there until we decide what to do with you." They appeared to be discussing just that–what to do next. Even at a distance, Wade was intimidating. He had refined the attitude.

"It took me days to get here. I'd rather not be standing out in the rain." He looked up at the overcast sky for emphasis. "Or snow."

After a few minutes, several more people joined the group and four of them made their way down the road. "That's him," one of the men said, recognizing Wade. Luckily for him, it was someone he'd rescued days earlier rather than someone he'd crossed paths with in January. A few of those Nomads might still be wandering nearby.

"You've been playing guardian angel to some folks traveling here," the first one to call out to him said. "Do you have business in Skyline?"

"Nothing I'd care to discuss on the street," Wade said. "I'm here because I was told this is a haven. I'm tracking a band called The Sixth." Both references triggered subtle responses from all four. Two went defensive and two didn't.

"Which clan of The Sixth?"

"I don't know. How many are there?"

The man shrugged. "They're secretive, hidden, so we don't really know. Dozens, maybe. Any clues, because you're in for a long search, otherwise."

"The clan that stays up north, near the old state line," Wade said.

"There are three larger clans affiliated with The Sixth that far north. We can't give you much direction concerning them. Some travel with the expeditions, as they move in the summer. It's safer." He extended a hand. "I'm Giles." Tall, leaning towards gaunt, he was past fifty, a shock of abundant white hair and animated dark eyes. "You're welcomed to stay. This is a haven."

"I'll stay for a few days and see what my options are." He shook his hand. "Wade."

"Are you an auditor for Councilor Vance, or any Councilor? I have to ask, because if you are, you have to inform me. It's a law."

Wade collected his weapons and gathered the reins up. "No, I'm not. I've met Vance. Now I want to meet The Sixth."

Giles chuckled. "Like I said, there are a few of them, out and about in the mountains. Figure out which clan, or hope they're as curious about you as you are about them."

"I never got the chance to thank you," the refugee he'd saved offered. "My sister and her family. We didn't know what else to do."

"I didn't do it for the thanks, I did it for those kids. Are they here?" Wade asked.

"They are, and doing well. The three oldest will be starting school in a few days," the man explained, sounding as if it were something he never expected would happen.

"Do you have any contact with The Sixth?" Wade resumed speaking to Giles.

"No, we're a haven."

Wade gave a half-hearted shrug, indicating he didn't understand the reasoning. "I'm not from the area."

"We're not allowed to purposely contact The Altered."

"Altered? That's a law?" Wade asked, more amused than alarmed. "I'm looking for The Sixth."

"We could lose our haven status, be fined, sanctioned on the trade routes, the list goes on, if any of the Councilors happened to have an auditor who caught wind of it. The Sixth are The Altered. Oh, not everyone, but enough." Giles explained. "Genetic experiments from before the war. They aren't just urban legends."

"Huh," he offered, looking skeptical.

"You've met one. Vance is an Altered, but not the same as The Sixth."

"I thought the havens deemed them illegal. He's running things, up in Estes Park."

"He's the exception." Giles let it go at that, not wanting to have a deep political discussion, out in the rain, with a stranger.

"They wouldn't hear it from me, if you let someone from the clans know I was here."

"We'll see," Giles said.

The road wound uphill, cresting, revealing a wall, and beyond that, a village that looked almost like something from a hundred years earlier. Compact, well-maintained homes, newly tilled gardens, people going about their day. The only thing standing out was the fact the homes were sheltered, many partially underground. Insulation from the cold and from damage raiders might try to inflict.

"It's not as if we can keep track of every Altered that wanders the range. I'm certain they come to Skyline for supplies, now and then," Giles continued.

"Now and then," Wade agreed. "That's good. I don't want to be here all summer, waiting. I have business up north, too."

"Vance," Giles thought.

"Farther north," Wade repeated. "This year, I hope. Or west." Exploring the far west had always been a goal, even when it seemed improbable. Now that he was working alone, there was nothing to hold him back.

***

Several older men were speaking among themselves as JT accompanied Shan to the sparsely decorated office. From what she'd been able to observe, Shan was convinced that she was either not in Angelfire, or it had been exaggerated in the stories she'd heard. The handful of buildings didn't account for a major city. Either way, a great ploy.

Any of the men could be related to Hunter. She'd known who JT was long before they met in person. Not so, in this instance.

"These are Assembly members. They don't bite, but keep in mind what I said," JT coached her as they made their way inside. "Chair Philip Caulder, this is Capt. Shannon Allen," he spoke to the gray-haired man who came to greet them. He introduced the other two as well.

"Sir," she spoke politely to each. The other two excused themselves, heading back to the city, they said.

"Captain," Caulder acknowledged, getting right to his concerns. "I should be alarmed at someone, even another Councilor, sending out a security force to keep tabs on me."

"I'd like to assure you, we had no intention of spying on Angelfire. We were out at West Mesa, sightseeing, because we could."

"Chase tells me you're quite tenacious, and tend to get your way. That you flew in here, in a blizzard, confirms his opinion. He also warned me we'd be having a visit from someone in Vista Security, before long."

Aware that Chase was Hunter's given name, she nodded. "Under the circumstances, my choices were limited to bad and risky. Councilor Vance isn't in my chain of command, and he's never asked me to spy on anyone. He lent me a map of refueling stations so I could do some reconnaissance. I've been working on my own for the past few weeks."

"I've talked to Vance. He's verified your story. He seemed impressed with your officers and spoke well of you."

Uncertain if he was joking, Shan confessed, "We don't always see eye to eye."

"He said as much, and blamed it on the generation gap. I've had a few reports about the Vistans. Apparently, being isolated has made you scatter across the states at the first opportunity. Your being here is unexpected, not unwelcome. Angelfire has accommodated a number of newly discovered towns and villages over the years."

"I'm certain our Council will be eager to establish communications with you."

"Vista Council or Cody Council?" A twinkle in his eye belied he wasn't all about business.

She smiled. "I doubt Cody has had the opportunity to establish a council. The Vista has, but I don't speak for them. They will be contacting you, through Councilor Vance, soon."

"Who do you speak for?" Caulder asked.

"Cody Security. In the future, maybe Vista Security."

"I appreciate your candor. Your Officer Taylor is recovering from surgery. Capt. Green has been at the hospital with him. I've arranged for you to contact your people, so they don't think you've gotten lost."

"We're overdue, but it's not a cause for alarm at this point. I've gotten lost before." Shan sensed the other councilors were observing them. Her.

"So I've been told. You have questions," Caulder didn't think otherwise.

"I've known about Angelfire since we arrived in Estes Park."

"Go on."

"This isn't it, this isn't the city," Shan said.

"No, it's not. This is an outpost. The hospital is here because it was before the war. We've made use of it for travelers. Same for the detention center. I have to imagine The Vista has similar precautions in place."

Shan nodded, listening.

"It's a defensive area," Caulder said. "That being said, understand you and your officers will stay here, as my guests. My decision is final until the Assembly has a chance to evaluate the incident."

"I'd like accommodations other than detention," she suggested. "One night without sleep I can manage, but it's been two running on in to three."

"I've heard you paced most of the night."

"She did," JT added. "I watched her."

"I've never been on that side of lockup. It hadn't occurred to me I'd have claustrophobia," Shan told them.

Caulder considered it. "There are quarters in the north wing of the jail. Our police use them as needed, but currently empty. I'm certain it's dusty, but there are full facilities. You and Capt. Green are welcome to use them until we sort this out. I'd also appreciate it if you let the Duty Office know where you're going to be, specifically, if you're not with one of my people. We'll speak again after you contact your superiors."

"Thank you, sir."

"Capt. Allen, we're not quite finished," Caulder said.

"Yes, sir?"

"Aren't you going to ask me about my son?"

A question she'd had time to contemplate. "I wasn't certain if it was appropriate."

Caulder understood her dilemma. "Keeping your personal life separate from your professional life isn't easy. It is appropriate, in this case."

"Hunter, Chase, was told not to expect anyone from Cody for months. Of course I'd like to see him and I'd be lying if I said it wasn't personal."

"He's not in the city. I'm having someone track down his expedition. You're due on a video conference with The Vista, if you're ready."

"Thank you." She hadn't expected such a quick response. They made their way to an interior room where the electronics were set up. She kept the thought to herself, that it was EMP hardened. Caulder, both of them, would question how and why she even knew what that meant. The radio tech exited, leaving them on their own.

"Capt. Allen, you're on the air," Caulder invited her to begin the conversation.

"Vista Home Base, this is Team Three, part one, Alert Six, over?"

"Go ahead, caller."

"Call word magic," she answered.

"Call word equator. Go ahead, Capt. Allen," whoever was at the other end said.

"Request you put the video online." The blank monitor went to static.

"It might take a few moments," the elder Caulder instructed.

The screen wavered and came up with two familiar faces.

"Cmdr. Niles, Maj. Dallas, this is JT Caulder and his father, Angelfire Assembly Chair Philip Caulder," she introduced.

Dallas was clearly ecstatic at seeing an old friend. "Senator Caulder," he greeted. "And Joey? I'd never have recognized you."

"Chairperson, now."

"We've all gotten demotions since the war," Dallas noted. Both of the older men laughed.

"I've always wondered how far you managed to get. There were search parties for a while," Caulder expressed with a touch of sadness. "Chase filled me in. I understand you're the old, married one now."

"That I am," Dallas agreed. "I hope we can all get together and share stories."

"We're working on that."

They chatted on for several minutes while Shannon took stock of more subtle things. Cmdr. Niles wasn't in Security Command; retired, running Dispatch. An interesting choice. She'd have picked someone less conspicuously a former military man, but then again, she wasn't home to see what had been happening in recent months. Dallas was a given. It was the first time she realized he didn't use his real name, either.

They all seemed at ease and talked for a time.

"If you'd like a few words in private, Capt. Allen," Caulder wrapped it up.

"Of course, thank you." She waited until they made their way out, aware the entire conversation was being recorded anyway. "How are things there, Dallas?"

"You remember, same things, different month."

"I get that," she said. Council and Command at odds, a normal state of things. It wasn't new or interesting. "Has Cmdr. Wade been checking in?"

"Like you'd expect him to."

Wade was off the map, then. No check in, no contact. "I've got nothing else urgent. Let Taylor's family know he's recovering. I'll be sending him back to Cody in a few days and he can talk with them then. Same for Green. Don't say anything to make my parents worry more than they already do."

Niles shook his head, taking mental notes. "Are you going to check in with Cody soon?"

"As I can, yes. If they call you first, give them the details. Cmdr. Niles, Maj. Dallas, I'll be in contact as I can. Cody has specifications, Call them if you have questions. Watch your back. Out." She kept it short. Neither had indicated how impatient Council might be getting. Mac was running interference for the team, then. Shan wondered how long he could manage it. A few more months, if they got lucky. Weeks were more likely, and if it was the same status quo, they were already on short time.

"And that's Councilor Caulder," JT told her, walking the short distance back to the jail. "He was more cordial than I expected, but he's like that with our sister. He can't help it. The Assembly will be intrigued by the idea of a new alliance with a new place. It's been a while."

"Are you interested in hearing my opinion?"

"Are these off-the-record?"

"Yes."

"If you feel safe divulging things to me. Extenuating circumstances. You know what I mean."

Shan knew he could have told his father at any point, what she was, and that it was a possibility in the future. Those extenuating circumstances happened more than she wanted to consider. "He doesn't automatically suspect someone is an Altered. I didn't expect that."

"Do you?"

"No," Shan told him the usual fabricated response. She sensed it, there was no guessing. The unique exception had been Rafe. "He's more trusting, too. Vance has him pegged as unyielding."

"With Vance, he's gotten that way, and he has his reasons. He's dealt with Altereds over the years that have made him less trusting and more unyielding than you think. You arrived here after our advisors informed him The Vista is a potential ally."

"Were you one of those people?"

"After what you did with Rafe, yes. I waited to form a solid opinion. Now, I have a question."

"All right, ask."

"When do you expect to hear from Wade?"

"He's out on his own, looking for The Sixth." Shan had thought he'd catch that bit of the conversation. It was a common question these days. She wished she knew.

"That's a thing best left unsaid."

"Wade wants to do this, he wants to be left alone."

"And what Wade wants, he gets," JT said.

"Yes, he does."

"What else about my father?" He didn't want to discuss Wade in depth, not with her, not with anyone other than his father. They were both worried about his motives, and how he would influence Team Three and the Angelfire Assembly.

"He values your opinion."

JT nodded. "I think my father likes you. He let you take over the training quarters. Outsiders don't get all the comforts of home because they smile at him."

Shan shrugged. "I only get one chance at making a first impression."

"What sort of first impression did you make with Vance?"

"It could have gone better. What do you plan on telling your father about Wade?"

"He knows a city the size of The Vista is bound to have a number of Altereds. When he asks for specifics about the offensive on Manitou Springs, the question will come up. It always does when they evaluate new haven prospects."

"I'm not at all comfortable telling him about me, and I won't tell him about Wade."

"Let your Council handle it."

"Council wasn't there."

"You've already made your report. Let them do the talking for you."

There were too many problems with that idea. "Council and Command will have a joint effort in this, I'm sure," she said. To the Vista Council, at least, The Altered might still be myth and speculation. Nothing good would come from the revelation that the rumors from before the war were true.

"Cody Base, this is Team Three, part one," Green called in, knowing they'd pick up sooner or later. It was after dark, but he'd hoped it would be sooner. They'd also understand the transmission was being monitored, because he was obviously not Shannon, call-name Team Three, part one.

"We spend more time reporting what we're doing than actually going out and doing things," Shan commented, standing next to him.

"Wade's found a way out of that," Green said quietly, their sentry standing out in the hall having a cigarette. "Going off the radar. Remember what I told you yesterday about tunnel vision? Still applies, maybe now more than ever."

She ignored the comment, not willing to admit she might be worried about Wade.

"Team Three, over," a voice coming through the weak signal answered.

"Call-word?" Green asked, not recognizing him.

"Onomatopoeia," Cody Base came back, stronger this time, and Ballentyne this time. "Go ahead, Team Three. Where are you?"

"Midnight," Green gave the call-word, then gave up his seat to Shan.

"We're in Angelfire," she answered, getting comfortable.

"What happened to the West Mesa plan?"

"Medical emergency, and because of a big storm, we didn't have the fuel to make it to Estes Park."

"What emergency?" Ballentyne asked, a more serious tone in his voice.

"Officer Taylor decided he didn't need his appendix anymore. He's recovering as expected, without it, and we are stuck here for now."

"Are you secure?"

"As much as we're going to be when we're not home."

"When will you be heading back?"

"That also remains to be seen. I've met with some official-type people. I might make a trip east, on one of the trade routes. It depends on how things pan out. You understand how that works."

"The primary goal of Team Three this season." Ballentyne understood what was happening. "See what you can."

"Of course it is," she told him. "I'll be sending Green and Taylor back soon."

"With protest from Green," Green added.

"Green has protested everything I've done for the past two days. Please note that," Shan told him.

"Done," Ballentyne said. "Anything else I should be aware of?"

"Update our people in Estes Park. Vance may have already. I'll see you in Cody," she told him. He knew when, he knew why.

"What was that?" Green asked.

Shan fidgeted in the chair. "I can't tell you."

Green was surprised. There wasn't much she didn't confide. "Are you sure?" he asked again.

"Never more certain, Damon. Plans have been moved ahead, nothing else."

"Sending us back to Vance defeats the purpose of being a team," he said, knowing it was basically pointless to argue with her.

"I'm not certain if it's back to Estes Park or back to Cody. Mac will have orders when you talk to him. His orders still override mine, and Wade's, until Wade sucks it up and goes to deal with

Command." She spoke low enough to keep the conversation one-on-one, even if the sentry was listening. Caulder hadn't been surprised, or alarmed, that they needed further use of the communications center.

"Got it," Green confirmed.

"Don't turn into Mac, and start worrying about it, because it won't change a thing."

He nodded, giving her that. Team Three wouldn't change their plans this far in.

"How long before Chris can safely travel?"

"Give it another three days without complications."

Shan did some calculating. "We can work with that. I have no delusions that we'll be invited to Angelfire itself, not this time."

"What are we going to do if our Council steps in and sends their own envoys?"

"There's a narrow window of opportunity this summer. We've already established with Vance. Here we are, as close to Angelfire as we can expect for now. The Sixth said to send diplomats, not soldiers, so I don't know how successful Wade will be."

"The point is, we're here and they aren't."

"They've hidden outside contacts from us, and they may have their own intermediaries in place already. I don't believe they do, yet."

"Which would mean they've cost Security lives," Green pointed out. "A damned good reason to want to keep their involvement a secret."

"It's out now. We'll find out for certain one of these days. It could mean Team Three's secret will be out, too. Cody needed to be a safe zone, in the event Council turns on us like we thought Caulder might."

"Do you wonder if that could happen?"

"The past year has changed everything. What do you think?" Even with her insight, sometimes she had to ask obvious questions. Sometimes, she turned the tables on him.

"When it comes down to it, people in The Vista are going to be loyal to each other. They are your family and friends. You were one of the first babies born there, after the war. They may not understand, and it might scare people, but we stick together. That's how we've survived. It's how we'll continue."

"The things I used to be afraid of aren't the things I'm afraid of now," Shan confessed. "Sometimes, I wish I'd stayed home."

"But not this time."

She agreed, nodding. "Not this time."

Chapter Eight

Skyline nightfall April 14

"No one volunteers for the overnight watch, but here you are, and looking like you enjoy it," Giles said. "You earned your room and board this week." He offered him a drink, and Wade nodded. "I won't even ask why, I don't want to be told stories about your life. As long as you want the job, it's yours."

The bar was getting ready to open. There would be a trickle of customers right away, followed by more as the evening wore on. The bartender, Lissa, shared the upstairs apartment with Giles. She was in her mid-thirties, and kept her dark hair short, a good look with her pixie-like features. Wade knew she carried a small caliber handgun on her hip, a big shotgun under the back counter.

It reminded him of wild west movies some evenings, especially when traders came in from the road. Her intent, as the place was Lissa's, and business was good. It was harmless noise from most customers. From the talk he'd heard, she'd seen worse. If he got the chance, Wade wanted to ask her about the overthrow ten years back, the one when they ran Rafe out of town. He hadn't dropped that name yet. Giles hadn't been involved.

Tonight, he was the quiet one. "I can't stay," Wade said. "I've told you, I'm hunting. It's important. If I get a lead, I'm gone. I'll give you as much warning as I can. It might be two hours, three days, or until the snow starts."

"Fair enough," Giles said. "If you meet them, The Sixth, here in the city, don't tell me about who they are. Say you're going to move on. It'll save both of us trouble later."

"The problem," Wade told him. "My friends are out here. We have a purpose, and one season before we run out of time."

"A bit of advice is in order. As long as you're working on your own, there's such a thing as freelance court officials. They patrol the outlying ranches and deal with any problems. The Sixth have stepped in, when we're lean on help. I can't pay them in Haven credits, but I make up for it in other ways. They take notice when we get new people, too."

"That way, you don't need to report me, or them, to an auditor that happens by."

"Bingo," Giles said.

"I don't mind day trips out. I can't do anything extended. Leaving you short-handed wouldn't be a good thing, either."

"Your call. The word is discretion."

"You've said that every day I've been here."

"It's important. The way I figure it, there are things you don't want me to know. Maybe not the same things I think they are, but it doesn't matter." Giles waved to Lissa. She grinned and waved back, taking orders from a group of workers seated next to the back door. "If anyone has a lead on visitors to the village you might want to talk to, it's going to be her."

"You don't mind if I discuss it with her?"

"Wouldn't have told you, if I did. Besides, she'd make me miserable if she heard otherwise. She can take care of herself."

"I believe you." There was a twinge of homesickness, of missing his team. His friends. Shan, insisting the same thing, that she could take care of herself, and always telling him to be careful. Mac, with his warped sense of humor and endless trivia of things from before the war. His mother, his sisters, even his step-father. Others, too, but them the most. If he thought about his children, he might toss the entire adventure out and just go home. Wanting them to live a life where they didn't have to worry about their past, their bloodlines, kept him moving. He had a drink.

It was hours later before the crowd thinned enough to strike up a conversation. "I've heard you're in charge of rumor control," Wade started.

Lissa smiled, shaking her head. "Everyone believes that, because I tend the bar. It's a silly stereotype, really."

"Giles told me."

"Did he? Giles imagines more happens here than does."

Wade nodded, taking the drink she poured. "I'm looking for the type of people that might not be welcomed here. If they were honest with you."

"Ah. We get all sorts through here, especially in the spring. I figure we might even have served a meal to the people who burned out that sonofabitch up in Manitou."

Wade just nodded again. "Trouble with raiders?"

"Not raiders, but I won't talk about that. Bad karma."

"That, I understand." Wade drank the shot. Whiskey, the old stuff.

"These people you're looking for. They could turn out to be worse than raiders." She thought about things long past. Wade could see it.

"That's what I need to know. I have friends who might be in danger."

Lissa had a drink with him. "If I hear anything, and if there aren't any auditors nosing around, I'll let you know." A younger woman made her way behind the counter to the back room. It was obvious they were related.

"Good enough, thank you," Wade said, watching the newcomer for a moment.

"She's not married."

"Excuse me?" Wade said, declining the offer of another drink. There were so many days he'd gone without alcohol, he'd pay for it in the morning if he kept indulging now.

"Chloe. She's not married, never has been."

"I'm a stranger in town. Why would you tell me that?"

"I've been told all about you. Talk about what you did for the Alma group gets around, then you followed them here. You've pointed out problems to Giles before they've cropped up." She leaned over the counter, voice low in the room's noise. "You might let those you meet think you're only a wanderer. I don't believe that."

"What do you think I am?"

"Honestly? I don't care. Actions, not opinions."

"Sister, or daughter?" Wade asked, meaning Chloe.

"That's cute. Flattery will get you nowhere. Chloe is my daughter, not Giles'. We have a seven-year-old son."

"I'm not looking for a relationship." In his opinion, they could pass for sisters.

Lissa shrugged. "Fair enough. Are you married?" She asked anyway, because Chloe had asked her days ago. She liked having those easy answers.

"No."

"I didn't figure it would hurt for you to meet people your own age. Get out and mingle. It's easier to talk to the travelers when you're with a group. They're cautious, and you've seen why. Chloe can introduce you to our regulars, at least. Get acquainted with a few people, gossip, make some friends even if it's temporary."

"Good idea."

"I thought so. Tomorrow she's working for me. After that, you'll have to talk to her about what she's doing."

"I will," Wade promised, heading back to sit with Giles.

"Now you see why she's the boss," Giles offered.

"I've got no problem with that."

"Me neither," he agreed. "That's how I like my happy home."

"As long as they don't get antsy and start moving, we'll meet the expedition by noon," JT said, not minding a brief journey out of the city. When he returned home, he'd be heading north to join Vance for the summer, if their yearly routine hadn't been changed by the appearance of the Vistans.

"It's safe for this few of us to be out here?" Shannon asked. Besides the pair of them, four armed soldiers escorting a courier east, making the entire group seven strong. She didn't want them to venture out on account of her. Caulder had insisted they weren't.

"Nothing is guaranteed. The routes are as safe as traveling out here gets."

It was the best chance she had to catch up with Hunter until he returned to Angelfire. From the talk, that could be months, and she didn't want to be stranded there. Otherwise, she might as well have headed north with Green and Taylor. Shan wanted to see him, and she wanted to ride the trade routes she'd heard so much about.

Out of habit, she adjusted her sidearm, the Sig she always carried, wondering about her recent decisions and how biased they could be. Councilor Caulder had brought up a dilemma. The personal aspect of her life started edging out the professional, if she was honest with herself.

"Are you concerned about your safety?" JT asked, seeing her fidget.

"No, not at all."

"You seem worried," he persisted. "That different perception you have scares me. You and Vance are nothing alike. I don't know how you act and react to a situation and I'd rather not find out. If there's a problem, I need to be aware now."

"Motivation. I wanted to do this, my partners too, and Hunter is out here. He's getting to see the big, wide world before any of us. Team Three pushed for it, and the rookie gets the first chance out." She felt the irony.

"You're not out here because he's an unsupervised rookie."

"No." Shan didn't supply details.

JT shook his head. "After all the talk from Vance, he had me convinced Team Three was waiting around to make a move on the Havens. Even after I talked to Chase, I didn't know what to expect."

"If anyone in The Vista was aware of the Havens, it'd be a surprise to me." She had doubts, but those would be taken up with Council, later, if at all. "Last summer, after Rafe started testing our defenses, we got the idea we might have ventured across some invisible line and pissed someone off."

"That, at least, is accurate enough."

"You can ask me, about me." His curiosity was obvious to her.

JT nodded, knowing it was the only offer as he'd get.

"What else did he tell you?" she wondered.

"A lot less than you imagine."

Shan didn't understand.

"That's between brothers, Capt. Allen. Ask him, in an hour."

"I will," she said. An interesting conversation, no doubt. Maybe she didn't want to know, having heard talk between men at the station.

They could hear the noise of the camp before it came into view. Indistinguishable voices, movement, restless horses, all the sounds of a clear spring day. Shan broke out in a spontaneous smile, urging her horse into a trot for the last half mile to camp. JT kept up with her.

"Caulder," the sentry recognized him, catching the horse's bridle as they stopped behind one of the makeshift corrals. "What brings you to Colorful Colorado?"

"Unofficial visit," JT said, taking a note from him. They were expected.

"We're in Colorado?" Shan asked.

"You said something about invisible lines earlier. Borders. We're pretty close to one now, one we take seriously enough to have markers all along the way. A team checks those markers every time an expedition passes."

"No wandering away to see the sights."

"Not here." He asked the sentry, "Have you seen my brother today?"

"Ah, the new one. He's helping Gin and the others with the big tent, out in the clearing."

"Bring your gear, we'll have tents set up all along the trail. Yours will be up front where the sentries and forward riders are," JT motioned for her to join him. Shan followed, pack over one shoulder and a .223 long rifle over the other.

"How far are we from Texas?" she asked as they followed a dirt path up the hill towards what she guessed was the main area of the encampment. Not midday yet, she had plenty of time to survey her surroundings.

"Sixty miles."

"I see."

"It's something you need to be aware of."

"Noted," she said, Vance's warning about Texas fresh in her thoughts. "I get it. I won't wander off."

Having dealt with a sister about her age, JT let it go. Young women did what they pleased, and older women smiled their approval.

A couple dozen people were busy setting up tents and moving supplies into the larger one. A few sat on the side of the path, unpacking guitars to entertain a crowd later. One of them was Hunter, concentrating on tuning the strings, and unconcerned about the gathering audience.

A man and woman started playing and several people clapped in rhythm to the tune. He joined in, out-of-tune or not. No one seemed to notice. They were enjoying the early break in travel, and the decent weather.

"Relax," JT whispered. "We're safe here, as long as you are

heading east, keep to the marked route. It goes across places in eastern Colorado and western Kansas." In case she decided to see the sights.

She nodded acknowledgment as others joined in the singing. Hunter glanced around at the gathering crowd. Then he glanced around again, seeing JT first. He saw her, too, smiled for a moment, then returned to the song without missing a note.

"Is that the greeting you expected?" JT asked, still figuring out what sort of man his brother was. One thing he was certain of, Caulder men were drawn to headstrong women.

"It is," she admitted. "We're careful, about everything we do, especially in public. This is in public, as far as I'm concerned, and as far as he's concerned."

"Meaning you and Wade."

"Meaning anyone on a team. Besides the fact that he's a rookie and I'm a senior officer." Shan had her own bout of smugness. "That was a joke."

"Great," JT said as the song ended and the crowd broke out into applause.

"And I'm the one who needs to relax?"

Hunter joined them, guitar in hand. "Joey, Shan," he said, a lot of questions in mind. "Why are you here?" Before either could answer, he caught her arm, pulled her close and kissed her. Short and to the point.

Shan leaned in to whisper. "I'm not here just because you are, I'm here because my team needs me to be. You can help me, or not. Your call." Short and to the point. "I'm going to drop my gear in my tent," she told them both.

JT was wearing a wolfish grin as they watched her walk away. "What did she say?"

"None of your business," Hunter said. "Why did you bring her here?"

"You don't have the means to bribe me for that story. Ask her yourself."

"Good idea."

"She's going to wreck you," JT observed.

"Yeah. I'm going to enjoy every minute of it, too" Hunter decided. "I'll see you tonight."

"If you're lucky."

Hunter caught up with her as she was checking tags on tents. "D3," she told him, showing him the bit of paper the sentry passed along.

"Third row, alphabetical. Why are you here?" he repeated.

"Command wants someone on the trade routes."

"Naturally, that would be you."

"We weren't going to make contact until later in the year. Command and Council are still fighting over what baby steps out of that valley, towards here, we should take next. But yes, it's me. I seem to have some sort of influence over the Caulder men."

"How's that?"

"Your father gave me permission to join the expedition, and JT volunteered to show me out here."

"You got my father to let you come out here?" He thought he'd start out simple, because nothing she did was ever simple, or uncomplicated.

"He's been talking with Vance. Honestly, I think they'd both rather I be out of the way than standing in their office, wanting to know everything about everything we don't know."

"I'm sure there were conditions."

"I sent Green and Taylor Two back to Estes Park with the promise that someone with a little more authority than me would be in contact from The Vista."

"That's it?"

Shan found her tent. Two rooms, the outer one with a skylight. "He thinks I'm a lowly security officer, and he's right." She inspected her new living space. It was clean, and dry. Good enough.

Hunter followed. "Don't tell me you flew in during that storm last weekend."

"Fine, I won't."

"You did, though?"

"Green did the piloting. I just sat there, picturing how I was about to die."

When he realized she wasn't kidding, he stifled any snide remark. "Why?"

"Short version – Chris got sick and we ran out of options when the weather turned. If Angelfire didn't answer, we were going to ditch it as close to one of the refueling stations as we could, and call for help from there." Shan sat her gear in a corner and got a canteen out for a drink.

"You're not wearing body armor," Hunter observed. What she was wearing – black button-up jeans, black boots, her Sig, a long-sleeved gray flannel shirt and a short camo green parka, unzipped – was a good look for her. He thought so anyway.

She glared at him, dropping her canteen and clamping her mouth shut instead of saying something rude.

He knew that look. "And you're pissed at me. Because I kissed you?"

For a moment, Shan was astonished. "You think that's why I'm angry?" She put her hands on her hips, only stressing the fact she was mad, and that she wasn't wearing body armor.

"Apparently, no. What did I do wrong?" Hunter asked, leery.

"You could have asked me to come with you, when you left Estes Park."

"You told me not to."

"I might have alluded to it. The point is, you should have asked," she said her peace. Hunter wasn't like the other men she knew, the ones she'd grown up around. She had no trouble expressing herself to the select few of Team Three's inner circle, or talking them in to things.

There was no winning the argument. "What about Mac?" he expressed his own frustration.

"Mac?" she repeated, puzzled.

"Tall guy. Wears a cowboy hat, watches a lot of old movies when he's off-duty. You two are ... involved."

She sighed. "I forget, sometimes, that you think my relationship with Mac has some bearing on my relationship with you. It doesn't."

"Maybe not for you," Hunter corrected. "And maybe not for him. I have trouble working around that. Once I figure it out, I'll tell you all about how I feel."

"I don't even know how to respond," Shan decided after a moment.

"What do you need my help for?"

"I'm a Scout, I might as well see what I can about this trade route. It might keep Command from firing me, later."

Hunter folded his arms, never sure if she was joking when it came to Command.

"There are times I really despise that ... smug look," she folded her arms, daring him to respond.

He held his ground, silent.

"No, I don't know if Command will fire me. They might. It doesn't mean I'd be out of Command, only Security. It means I'd be free to do what I wanted, when I wanted. Right now, they own me," she shrugged, knowing he was aware of her position, and why she kept it.

"There it is," Hunter said. "You're here, on orders. Pretend you're not, because that's part of the job. And yes, I'm happy to see you. I wasn't expecting to until damned near this winter, if I got lucky." Any further discussion about Mac was off-limits because he was their ace-in-the-hole. Hunter was aware of why they weren't together and it had everything to do with genetics.

"In the meantime," Shan went on. "You get to be my guide and tell me about the trade routes."

"This is the second time I've been out. The first was a five day trip to supply an outlying village. I'm not what you'd call a library of information. Talk to JT." The flaw in that line of thinking hit him even as he said it. "Or we can figure it out, together."

"Partners, then."

Hunter smirked, pleased at his sudden promotion. "Yes, ma'am."

"Looks like something is burning," Mac said, a thin line of smoke on the horizon, almost invisible in the morning light.

"All the damned time. They move fast, and we can never catch them." Harlan pulled a .243 from its scabbard and checked the road west. "Maybe it's nothing. We'll see." Easy-going, weathered around the edges, he was reserved, and soft-spoken, a change from his first contact. As he liked to say, he'd seen some shit over the years.

Mac had watched him go John Wayne on a gang of raiders, shouting and shooting at them. All the men from Black Hills had, scaring them off rather than an actual confrontation. It worked and Mac filed it away for future reference. Today, they were observing, half a dozen of them riding the old frontage road to the interstate.

"If they've been on the fringes for years, you'd think they know you aren't going to get caught off-guard, and they're just doing it to keep you on your toes."

"Yeah, that," Harlan agreed. "When we first set up in Dakota, we thought they were testing our defenses. It looked that way. It still does. No one takes fifteen years to plan a raid." He put the rifle away. "It's a band from one of the clans, playing games."

"You know Rafe watched The Vista longer than that."

"You know, Rafe was a fucking lunatic," Harlan pointed out, a bit of sarcasm in his voice.

Mac nodded, contemplating his words first. "Until October, we weren't aware what we were up against. The Sixth we met told us what he was. The Altered part, not the fucking lunatic part."

"Not Vance? You've got to be kidding."

"No, not ever, not about that."

"I watched him, watching you, for years."

"Vance, or Rafe?"

"Rafe. Vance didn't have that sort of interest in hunting Altereds."

"You were with the group that came to Colorado, right after the war." Mac knew he was, he just wasn't sure if it was relevant now. "What did Vance do?"

"They fought, all the time, about everything. A power struggle, and most of us had the sense to step back. We should've run like hell, but we'd already considered our options, and there weren't many, not after August, when the snow started and didn't stop. People were dying fast, before they realized they were sick. This continent didn't escape the war, either. We didn't know, when we went to sleep at night, if we'd wake up the next day."

Harlan fell into thought, silent for a time. "After Rafe figured out what was happening in Montana, it got worse. The original clan split up. I headed north, thinking it would be far enough."

"He wanted to get rid of potential competition. Including my partners, when they were children."

"I don't have any idea what his motives were. There was in-fighting, still, after we went our separate ways. Some of them finally traveled north to see."

"This was when?" Mac questioned, having a horrible suspicion.

"Twelve years ago, when it got closer to autumn. Four of them came back, Rafe and Vance, naturally. They wouldn't talk about it, but we heard things. All hell broke loose before winter set in and we went defensive on each other. It took Rafe a lot of years to hunt down Moore. He thought he'd get the northern routes. He didn't. We have four of them in the Dakotas, but they're good, secure ones."

"What happened to Yates?"

Chuckling, he said, "You know, Wade didn't have to ask."

Mac jumped to conclusions, thinking that Wade had sent someone to watch over him like he was a rookie. "You're with The Sixth?"

"Not even in the most remote way. I'm Yates."

Mac considered the implications. "Wade has been looking for The Sixth."

"And I'm certain he'll find them. He found us first. I use my given name now, because there are people around who still remember there was a bounty on Yates."

"Yates, the one not an Altered."

"True. I've worked with them all my life, and I have a handful in my employ. After you blew the side out of a pretty big mountain in the middle of Colorado, it kind of got our attention." Harlan had never been one to pull punches. "We planned to see Vance in person. Wade caught us before we crossed the border. Saved us a trip to the city."

"He sent you to Cody?"

"Wade may be the big boss in Montana, not here. He didn't tell me to do anything. He told me about Cody, a little about The Vista, and said you might need a hand. Since you're right up the road ..."

"Three hundred miles," Mac added.

"I figured Rafe was right to worry what you'd do, when you were old enough to care. I'm interested in helping you move towards doing those things. Not the Havens Caulder has established. Those aren't necessarily safe if you're an Altered, or a former ally."

"We want to establish contact there, too."

"He'll let you. Their laws don't apply to you unless he says so."

"Selective enforcement?"

"Let's just say Caulder's word is law. It's his city."

"Are we in danger from him? Meaning The Altered among us."

"Not as long as you're representing The Vista. He's smart, don't get me wrong. Blaming The Altered for everything bad that's happened since the war, well, he has his reasons. Let him think he's right."

"That's setting up a lot of lies to establish a treaty with someone," Mac said. "I wonder if it's worth it."

"Is that up to you?" Harlan asked.

"As far as Cody is concerned, it is. Vista Council will form their own opinions."

"What's their stance on The Altered?"

The pair rode on, well ahead of the loud quartet of their friends, Mac contemplating before he answered. "The Council has no stance on The Altered. As far as I can tell, the idea is something that died during the war." They followed the road as it curved back towards the city.

"And your Security Command?"

"They've always known." Mac kept it to himself that he believed some members of Command were indeed Altereds. He decided they found a way to hide themselves.

"Will they back you if the time comes? Civilians getting involved has a way of making a situation blow up into a disaster, and we both know it could happen, even in The Vista."

"It's just my opinion, but yes, they would."

"I hope you never need to find out," Harlan said.

"Now you understand why Cody is so important to us."

"Your stance on The Altered should be one of caution, at any rate. They're not all like Wade and Allen. They're not all like Rafe, either."

Mac nodded. "My stance on everyone is caution."

"I rode right in to Cody."

"We'd been watching you screwing around outside our perimeter for weeks. I had an idea what you were doing."

"That's the other thing we should talk about," Harlan broached the subject. "Being isolated, and then your only outside information coming from Vance, we should discuss what sort of Altered you are."

"I've never said I was."

"If you were, and the sort Rafe couldn't sense, that would be more than a little unusual. We knew about Wade and Allen because he picked them up as soon as they hit puberty."

"Does puberty have anything to do with it?" Mac wondered.

"No. He knew none of the others would go along with a plan to hunt down children because he'd tested the idea before. It didn't stop Rafe. He sensed two active Altered, suspected three, and counted a number of other inactives. Those numbers are high, compared to averages that have been documented across other areas since the war."

"How many?"

"I'm not one of them. They didn't confide in me."

Mac stopped his horse and dismounted, letting the animal rest up a bit. Harlan joined him, walking up the trail, horses following. "Does Vance or Caulder have files on them?"

"Caulder, no. Vance, there's no way of knowing. Any information Vance has would have come from Rafe. If either of them kept information other than in their heads, it would be the two they were concerned about, not dozens that will never realize they are different."

"Allen is female," Mac offered, to see his reaction, to see if there was a lie. He had sensed nothing to cause alarm.

"Yes, I could tell. I've observed her, and both of them, at various times. I suspect you are the third for that reason. You're their partner, and that choice wasn't made lightly."

"A Security matter, nothing more. Besides the fact, I started Team Three." Mac still sensed nothing deceptive in his tone. "Until a few summers ago, the only consideration we had was for The Vista. Until we had Scouts confirming other villages, we were the center of the universe."

"That's a dangerous way to live," Harlan said.

"It kept us safe for two decades."

"Does the term 'fourteenth' mean anything to you?"

"Vance called them the fourteenth. He had a brief and unhelpful explanation of it."

"None of you are geneticists, so there's that."

"As far as anyone is concerned." Mac let him think it was a joke. He had a good idea who he was talking to the next time he visited home. Wade's mother had worked on The Altered project, unaware of the ulterior motives.

"The freelance Altered, the ones that slipped away, the ones they lost contact with or control of. They're called The Wildblood. They have little training and less use of their abilities. Some of them have shown abilities not on record."

"What sort of abilities?"

"Acute sensory perception, synesthesia, telepathy, others that don't have names." Harlan shrugged. "Things I can't even imagine."

Mac looked skeptical. "If any of those were true, do you think I'd tell you?"

"Not for a second. I might recognize it, if someone meant to conceal their abilities from me. It's not as simple as you might imagine. Wade has kept a specific group of people around him for years. Why is that?"

"For security, for the safety of everyone in The Vista. Are you suggesting other Altereds follow similar tactics?"

"I'm not suggesting anything, I'm plain telling you they do. It's an instinct, and it's as old as human existence. The Altered are more in tune with their natural instincts. Humans seem to have outgrown it over the past few centuries."

"Now The Altered are feral?"

"Not at all. That instinct makes them adaptable, intelligent, and dangerous. They might, oh, watch a potential ally for days or weeks, assessing them."

"Or they might deny being Altered, in favor of being the struggling human, to throw off the curious," Mac countered.

They continued on in silence for a while as the others caught up again, then they moved on ahead, eager to get back for the night. Mac had the same interest in Black Hills as Harlan did in Cody. For now, his place was there. Maybe he'd send Ballentyne east.

"I'll be a lot happier when Shannon gets the order to move the team back here," Mac said. "Capt. Allen, I mean. Letting this business in Estes Park go on is asking for another problem, like the one in Manitou. It doesn't matter that Vance knows us."

Harlan stopped, an edge of caution in his voice. "You need to check in with Estes Park. Capt. Allen isn't there. In fact, we can't verify where she is. I assumed you'd have been notified if a team went missing by accident."

"Bennett," Mac yelled at the riders in front of them. "Get that radio out and get me on with the com center five minutes ago." Command, he knew, was responsible for whatever he wasn't being told. He didn't intend on mincing words with them.

"Cmdr. MacKenzie, we were beginning to think you'd gone and headed south to do freelance work," Duncan greeted, caution in his voice.

"My first responsibility is here," Mac replied. "I was aware Wade was in southern Colorado. Where have you sent Shannon?" They were on radio only, no video. He'd told them weather conditions were causing communications problems. The truth was, he got a better sense of what they weren't saying, when they were only speaking. The video feed distracted him.

"It was an unplanned change. Due to these unforeseen circumstances, her assignment has been adjusted. Green and Taylor are back in Estes Park. Capt. Allen is out-of-contact, her last known location at Angelfire."

Harlan was in the lobby with a couple of his men, curious about the conversation happening behind soundproof and bullet-resistant plexiglass. Mac had an outstanding poker face and was using it.

Mac swore out loud to himself, angry. "Angelfire is considered hostile territory."

"We're aware of the designation, since we set it," Duncan said.

"My point is, Capt. Allen may not be aware of the situation there. Is it possible to send a team back out with her?"

"At this time, no," Perro spoke this time. "I understand your concern. Lt. Hunter is in the same location."

"I sent him there," Mac came back. "Personal feelings aside, I've never been comfortable with single officers wandering the outlands when we know so damned little about what to expect."

"If anyone can start a conversation with Senator Caulder, Capt. Allen would be our best hope. Yes, because of her relationship with Hunter. We didn't specifically discuss it, but she's a smart young woman, and she understands that, too. The reason we're telling you is that when either of your partners makes contact again, you're a more likely candidate than we are." Perro understood of how independent the entire team had become since the discovery of life outside The Vista. Command knew how they'd respond. It was why they hoped it wouldn't happen for a few more years. The older the team, the more mature they'd be, and the more reasonable. In theory.

"There were protocols already in place," Mac said.

"Cmdr. Wade is indisposed or ignoring our predetermined contacts. Capt. Allen isn't a full day late yet, but at this point, we don't expect her to keep to the schedule, either." Perro paused. "Have you heard from them?"

"I have not," Mac said. Not on the radio, not any other way.

"If you have the opportunity," Perro said. "The time is coming for Team Three to report to Command in person. That report will include an explanation to Council as well."

"Security isn't accountable to Council," Mac started on an argument as old as The Vista itself.

"No, they aren't. When multiple incidents happen within our perimeter, within the city, it's time to step up and let Council voice their fears. Everyone else in Command knows it, and that includes you now. I expect you to pass on the message to your team. But yes, whatever decisions about Security that will be made are still at the discretion of Command. All of Command."

Mac paced, attempting to choose his words as carefully as Wade would. "Are all members of Team Three still active Command officers?"

There was a brief silence. "Wade is considered unaccounted for, but he is an active member. So are you and Capt. Allen. I don't foresee your status changing."

Mac nodded to himself. "The three of us?"

"The three of you," Perro repeated.

"We tell Council our story and answer their questions."

"Alleviate their fears. Command will discuss this prior to any event with Council, of course."

"Does Command have any intention of changing security in Cody?" It was their backup plan. He needed to be certain.

"Not unless a request is made by Cody Security."

He couldn't detect any tension in Perro's voice. He was also aware the commander had been dealing with the team before they became a team.

"To reiterate," Duncan added. "When Wade and Allen call in, get them in and get yourselves to The Vista. This needs to be taken care of before the season is over."

"Understood," Mac said. "I'll try to get them moving."

"Don't try, do," Duncan told him.

"You gave us Cody for a reason," Mac said. "Let us do what we're here for while we can. A few weeks aren't going to change what happened. Summer is short. We'll be home before the weather shuts travel down. This is new to all of us. You might think about giving us some leeway."

"The problem with Team Three is that we've given you free rein from the beginning. You have your orders."

Chapter Nine

Colorado nightfall April 18

"Feeling better?" Hunter asked, taking a seat next to Shan, in the last row of the mess tent.

"We spent three days trying to catch up with the expedition." She'd had a long nap for most of the afternoon. As a guest of the Senator, she had little else to do. If she considered her job in Command, she'd be out surveying the area, except for the rain. Rain could turn to ice fast, this early in the year.

"I'm happy you're here," he went back to their earlier conversation. If she was in the right company, she said what she was thinking. Here, she was bound to be cautious. He had been, too, a habit he couldn't break.

Dinner was fresh venison stew with potatoes and onions, bread still warm from the oven, and beer cold from sitting in the creek. The scent of the campfires, and the food permeating the air, the quiet calm, the lack of urgency, all made the entire camp seem comfortable. Safe.

"I'm not on a particular schedule. We'll be heading for The Vista soon." She'd decided to take a break, to rest and relax for the day. Security wasn't her concern for a while.

"All of us, or Team Three?"

"All of us. Junior officers will be exempt from having to deal with Council."

"Council, great."

"Pretend you weren't expecting it."

"When are you going?" he asked, knowing if there was an order, it had been ignored or she wouldn't be here.

"When I have no other choice."

"I ended up in front of Command and Council Chair Haines as soon as we started working together," Hunter mused. "Looks like we're doing that again."

"Sounds like a good story," JT said, wandering in. The mess tent was the first place he'd looked for them. "Join me at my campfire and tell me the rest. I've brought beer as an offering."

"We can do that," Shan said, finished with the meal. She stacked her dishes on the pile and waited for them. "I bet there will be some interesting embellishments." Her trust in JT was as good as it was going to be until she'd known him a long longer than a few days. It would be interesting, to see what he had to say, and how he'd react.

"I don't exaggerate," Hunter defended, following his brother and holding the door open for her. She still wasn't wearing body armor. There was a Sig on her shoulder, like he'd expected.

Shan grinned at them. "Please, do tell." It was a short walk along the trail, passing other campfires, and groups of people enjoying the evening. There was music and laughter.

"Let me know if I get close to anything classified," Hunter added, finding canvas chairs already waiting.

She shook her head, gesturing for him to continue.

JT took a seat on the other side of her, passing out the beer. Two for each. "There's plenty more, but keep in mind, we break camp at daylight."

"I'm not talking about the Sweeps run at the end of April," Hunter warned, back on the subject.

"No," Shan agreed. "We got called up to Command when we came back from following Wade to Colorado. Or trying to follow Wade to Colorado. Someone had different orders, ones that superseded mine, and ones he didn't tell me about until later."

Hunter shrugged. "That was the second time we worked together, and 'bam', this close to a reprimand on my record."

Shan laughed. "I've heard about your time with the caravans. Don't act like you'd never been in trouble before."

"Second time out," he repeated.

"Is that how you two met, with the caravans?" JT asked.

"He hasn't told you?" she asked.

"Capt. Allen, you're a mystery to me. I asked my brother how many women he was involved with and he said, just one, when she's ready to be serious."

Shan raised her eyebrows, savoring the beer. It was dark and rich and cold. "And you think he meant me."

"He has spoken your name. I recognize that look of someone infatuated. Infatuated and terrified."

"You were worried about me embellishing stories," Hunter said, settling back.

"Did you say that?" Shan expected an excuse.

"Yes, I did." Hunter drank some beer. If there were going to be drunk confessions, he intended to fully participate.

"How did you meet?" JT repeated, curious.

"A year ago," Hunter said. "We met a year ago last week, on a road, in the middle of the night. She ordered me to get the hell out of her way. When we actually met face to face, she told me I drove like shit and that rookies shouldn't be allowed out to play."

"Sort of accurate," Shan gave him that one. "Letting a rookie drive at night, on that road. Questionable."

"I'll let Dallas know, next time I talk to him," Hunter countered.

"Pretty sure I already told him."

"You're not joking about being his senior officer?"

"He's been in Security two years. I've been in Command that long, Security since I was fifteen."

"What does a fifteen-year-old do in Security?"

"I sat in the com center except on field training days. It didn't take me long to qualify as a Dispatcher. I'm close quarters qualified, too. I drive, mostly, and mostly by myself."

"On the ice, in the dark," Hunter added.

"When did you tell him about that unspoken thing?"

"When she had to. When we were following Wade to Colorado. She didn't want to, and couldn't prove a thing," Hunter said. "She was sick, and I was done playing around."

"Trust issues. Every person like you I've run across has those in spades."

"From what I've seen, with damned good reasons," Shan said. "No disrespect intended, but death threats are a real thing for us."

JT nodded, agreeing.

"When I got her to go home, we were sent right to Command. At least I knew why. Then they gave us Cody. The rest," he shrugged.

"A fabricated tale."

"No comment," Shan added.

"I'll bet you say that a lot."

"I don't have to. Very few have seen anything that would indicate I'm different. Most of them don't even realize it, if they see something unusual."

"How would I tell?"

"She'd never let you," Hunter said. "I had to resort to bribery."

"Yeah, there are some things I don't want to know."

"You have a dirty mind," Shan pointed out.

"All men do, Shan. If you don't know it now, you'll figure it out soon," Hunter mugged it up for her.

"What's next?" JT meant both of them.

"I don't want to ride the trade routes all summer," Shan confessed. "I mean, I can't. Councilor Caulder offered this time, and

I accepted. Groups head back every week or so, and my time here has to be limited."

"Why?" Hunter made it a simple question.

She hesitated. JT was one of Vance's advisers, and anything she said could get back to him damned fast. "We have to go back soon. Home. The Vista."

"This is all about Wade, isn't it?" Hunter knew. It was a Team Three thing. Wade was their leader, unofficial or not.

"I'm not going to talk about Wade."

"I can leave," JT offered. "I mean, this is my campsite."

"It's not because of you. Team Three doesn't talk about Team Three to anyone," Hunter explained.

"That's a rough way to live."

"There are three or four other people they confide in."

"And you're not one of them."

"Like it or not, he is, at least for me," Shan said. "I have to get back to Estes Park because I left a group of rookies there. Wade is ready to regroup in Cody, and I need to be there with them when he does."

"Wade doesn't trust Vance?" JT asked.

"You've missed the entire conversation," Hunter told him. "Wade doesn't trust anyone not Team Three or one of his chosen. I'm not one."

"I say you are, so you are."

"According to you. It's not unanimous."

"You work for Vance. I have a lot of issues with that," Shan told JT, ignoring Hunter.

"I have for the past six summers. The Angelfire Assembly has indicated my time there is at an end."

"That won't make him suspicious," Hunter said.

"Our advisors change often. He might read nothing in to it, because I mentioned it last year."

"Here's hoping."

"I've done what Command wanted, to make contact with

Angelfire," Shan said. "I should consider this my vacation, because once I get back to Cody, I won't get that opportunity again soon."

"Do it, then," Hunter urged. "You'll know when it's time to clear out of Estes Park. Until then, take a break."

"I think I'd get bored."

"No, I won't let you get bored."

"Is that a promise?" Shan asked.

JT snorted his opinion, looking around for another beer. "If my brother lets you get bored, find the Quartermaster. He'll send you up front to do some scouting. It won't be anything as exciting as you're used to, but at least you won't be bored."

"I'll give it a few days, and re-evaluate when it gets to be May," she decided. Or until she heard otherwise from either of her partners. She stood. "Are we drinking more beer?"

"We are," JT said. "Go straight up the aisle, back towards the mess tent. You'll see the commons area. We aren't on rations, get what you think we can drink tonight and still ride tomorrow."

"Don't challenge me like that," she said. "I've drunk bigger men down." A white lie. She was two beers in and had no intention of giving in so soon.

"But could you climb on a horse and gallop on down the trail when you were done?" Hunter drawled. Both men laughed.

"I don't get it."

They laughed even harder. "Get more beer, woman. The Caulders are going to show you how they drink until they're stupid," JT announced.

"This isn't going in any report," she decided, shaking her head and wandering off to find more beer. Maybe they were right; she could use a vacation. Starting off rip-roaring drunk might not be the best idea, but it was the only offer she had at the moment. She found the supply tent and lugged a dozen bottles of ice cold beer back to the campsite.

Daybreak caught them all by surprise.

"The spirits must be restless today," the raven-haired Nomad commented, leading his horse to the water trough. It was early, with riders already congregating in preparations to get on the road. Mountains surrounded the area, but it was deceiving. Not far to the east, the Great Plains started and ran past the horizon, some five hundred miles.

The way station was neutral ground. Wade ignored him. Besides the fact that four more riders were making their way up the muddy path and he was there with Chloe. She'd gone in to the station. For the moment, the situation was under control. Lissa would kill him if he got her daughter in the middle of a senseless brawl.

"You never know what's going to wander in from the badlands this time of year," another one of them spoke up, stopping on the far side of the road, behind him, and effectively blocking off any chance of retreat.

Even in civilian clothes, Wade wore an over-abundant supply of weapons, and he discarded his parka on the saddle, to be sure the other men were aware. It was too early in the day to be dealing with idiots.

"Maybe the proprietors need to put up a new sign," a third pointed to the list of rules on a faded billboard. "One with pictures." He laughed along with his friends.

"If you have something to say to me," Wade spoke, careful not to raising his tone. "Say it, or shove off."

"We're only speaking to you if you're a piece of human waste, coming in to rob the trading post," the first answered, indicating Rule One on the billboard. 'Thieves Will Be Shot Without Questioning'. "This post is outside the haven boundaries, so you're on your own," he added to that train of thought.

"That works both ways," Wade pointed out. "Which is good for me. I don't have time to be waiting around for an inquest."

"Are you going to let him talk like that here?" another of the riders asked, fidgeting.

"Is there a rule against telling people to mind their own business? Because the world would be in a lot better shape if everyone did," Wade said.

"Problem is, I have business here, and since I haven't seen you before, I think you're that business," the first decided. "I thought I'd recognize you easier. Apparently not, but that's what happens. Maybe I'll explain it later, maybe I won't."

Wade didn't comment. He'd been seconds away from beating the daylights out of the entire band of The Sixth he was looking for, all this time, Kaden first. He still might.

"Did Lissa bring you here, or Chloe?" the one Wade had tagged as Kaden asked.

"Chloe is inside. Testing me like that is a bad idea. Don't do it again." Wade made it clear it was a threat.

"I won't have to. I'm Kaden."

"I know."

"We can talk here. Like I said, this is outside the haven. Spring rendezvous is this week, and people are moving. No one is going to take any notice of us unless we give them reason to."

"Do you always pick fights with people when you come here?" Wade waited for him to lead the way.

"Only when I want to see what someone is like. Shannon said you were the reasonable one. I suppose since you didn't shoot any of us, she's right." Inside the crowded trading post, he headed for the back, to the private dining rooms.

"I've never shot someone for having a loud mouth."

"You've found each other, I see," Chloe said, annoyed at their display. "I'm going to go check the vendors coming in. We'll be here for the night. Get rooms now, before they run out," she told Wade, not giving them a chance to change her plans. "You two should have plenty of time to get acquainted."

"We're familiar, friendly, nothing else," Kaden said, as soon as the door shut behind her.

"I could see that."

"That's one thing we need to discuss-how an untrained Altered can pull off using abilities you shouldn't even be aware of." Kaden stopped. "Unless all the information we've heard about you being untrained is fabricated."

"Not a bit," Wade said. "I figured out the basics from old media reports I dredged up at the libraries in The Vista."

"All on your own?"

"Shan, when she got a little older, had some added insights, but we've been alone in this. Our parents, our friends, co-workers, none of them seem to see, or maybe they don't want to. I created my own circle of trusted, to keep our secrets, in case someone did."

"Nothing to tell how you became aware."

"I just was, as far back as I can remember. So was she, and when I figured it out, I told her she wasn't alone."

Kaden nodded, taking a seat. His companions had gone their own ways. "Can we get whatever today's special is?" he asked a boy of about ten, who followed them to the alcove. The room was enclosed, with high windows, dark wood accents over freshly painted midnight blue walls, the electricity worked, and faint music reverberated from somewhere else in the building.

"It's the same special as it always is at this time of year-rabbit stew. Domestic rabbit, not wild. The wild ones taste better, but they're out-of-season. Fresh bread and butter, plus a vegetable. I don't remember which one. Do you want water, tea, milk, or beer to drink?"

"Tea," Kaden said. "The flavor that's already made."

"Milk," Wade answered.

"Goat or cow?"

"Goat."

The boy was making mental notes and hurried off to tell the kitchen. Returning in minutes, he balanced an array of bowls and plates on a platter he didn't seem tall enough to deal with. He passed the meal out, not spilling a drop.

"Maybe that's it," Kaden continued. "The two of you grew up together. You were close. Before the war, that didn't happen. The change of environment has triggered something they never expected, never documented."

"So the others, The Sixth, have abilities like ours?"

"I wouldn't say that. I'd say there could be similarities. Because of the vast amount of differences in genetics, even when the biotechs attempted to duplicate results, it never happened. Too many variables, and we weren't as smart as we thought we were. Humans, I mean. You and The Sixth? Time will tell."

"How's that?"

Sitting back, Kaden got comfortable. "When you're looking for an insight into what you are, do you think Vance is telling you anything that will make a difference?"

"It's no secret that I don't trust Vance. I don't trust you."

"It's not a secret. For now, I can tell you what I know about world events since the war. In exchange, I'd like you to give us the same opportunity you gave Vance, to prove we aren't your enemy."

"I'll give you that," Wade said. "Because I've already discussed this with my officers."

"With Shannon."

"I have other officers. Don't make me look bad by doing something stupid."

"I was going to say the same thing to you."

"Then we understand each other. Are my people safe with Vance?" Wade got right to business.

"Because he believes you and The Vista can give him the edge over other havens, yes, but only for now," Kaden said. "He's not as quick as Rafe to draw blood. That doesn't mean he won't."

"It's all about the trade routes."

Kaden nodded. "Of course. The trade routes mean we can survive and thrive. If you've studied any human history, it's clear.

Vance has the means to defend what he's built there. You know he has family."

"He never went into any personal detail, no."

"He does. You see what you've done to protect your family. Remember that, when and if the time comes."

"Do you think that could happen, that we'd have to run up against Vance like we did Rafe?" Wade didn't like the idea. Too many of those variables Kaden spoke of.

"Rafe had a few dozen men dug in. Vance has thousands of people. Most are civilians. Men, women, and children with no idea they're living on a powder keg. He's safe there, and he knows it. You know it."

"The Sixth-you're organized into at least one city."

"We have a dozen scattered camps of varying sizes, and our population fluctuates. Like you, like most places, we are composed of civilians and a handful of Altereds. I'm here to help keep you from becoming extinct."

"You two won't even notice if I wander back to Skyline on my own, will you?" Chloe asked, joining them for a few minutes. She wore her dark hair long and loose, suede leather riding pants with matching boots, and a high-collared denim shirt. The station was considered a safe zone, but she carried a hunting knife on her hip. There was a .22 Remington long rifle slung on the side of her saddle. She knew how to use them both.

"Of course we would," Kaden said, smiling at her "Make an order if you're hungry, and join us. This is likely to be the most eye-opening conversation you'll hear for yourself. Not rumor and innuendo, the real thing."

"The real thing?" Chloe repeated, intrigued. "Meaning?"

"An actual, live, untrained Altered, having lunch with us," Kaden offered and that earned her full attention. "A Wildblood."

"Is that true?" she asked, taking a seat.

"So I've been told," Wade said.

"It's true," Kaden verified. "And he's not alone."

"Technically, you're a Wildblood," she pointed out to Kaden. "Born after the war and all."

"Trained by a Sixth," he added a fact. "Devon Moore was a Sixth," Kaden said. "You're it, you're a Wildblood. I imagine Vance was pacing the floors when he found out."

"That's more than a little interesting," she said. "That's why you and Giles have been so secretive."

"We're not welcomed in some places. In a lot of places. I need Kaden to tell me the things I don't know, to protect myself and my home."

"That covers a lot of ground," she said

"Specific things," Kaden repeated.

"So you're a 'wildblood', or close to it," Wade repeated what Chloe said.

"I was raised with Altereds around me. I have training to control and enhance my abilities. In reality, not so much. Because of your isolation, that makes you a true Wildblood. Shannon, too, and any others in The Vista that meet those criteria. If they're adults and inactive, they'll stay that way. Untrained and aware equals wild."

"The others are unaware, and I won't be the one to tell them. No one will, because there's only one person who has a list, and she won't divulge."

"You are a commodity," Kaden told him. "Be careful."

"We're not so uncommon."

"Being untrained, you are. Some of us were wholly experimental, even for human genetic manipulation. The people that altered us had no idea what to expect. We have senses that there are no names for. My abilities differ from yours. Apparently, long-term contact as children allows some of those abilities to merge."

Wade kept a poker face, knowing this was true at least. "What was the reason for playing with human DNA to begin with?"

"There were a lot of reasons. They started out to eradicate diseases. Some corporations wanted to expand out in to space, and unaltered humans developed new diseases after any extended amount of time off Earth. There was that. And naturally, with the human propensity for destruction, there were groups who wanted super soldiers."

"What about the fourteenth?"

"There were a few progressive groups that wanted to improve the species in meaningful ways. They chose exceptional donors and added promising experimental procedures. Your guess about what happened next is better than most, because you've lived it."

"I've been told some frightening reasons behind that."

"Again, human ingenuity. What I told Shannon was the truth. Less than moral people influenced the trials. When they started developing their own race of humans, there wasn't much that could be done. Laws were ignored or bypassed. In the end, they thought they would control us like they had manipulated so many others," Kaden shrugged.

"They started a war to prove it," Chloe added.

Kaden went in for a brief history lesson. "Several wars that converged during the last year. A foreign power thought to get an upper hand by using biological weapons. By 'foreign power', I mean a government or corporate entity not on this continent. It escalated, it went nuclear. There wasn't enough time to create a cure for the strain that mutated, because it moved faster than they could track. Reports showed there may have been more than one strain. It didn't matter. It took less than three months for civilization to go out on Planet Earth. There's no way to account for how many wars happened in those last weeks. The power grids were the first things to go, and everything cascaded after that."

"They're still trying to control The Altered," Wade said.

"The havens are. This is why you need to reconsider your efforts to join up with their little clique. There are plenty of other ways for The Vista to make their mark, and to be safe."

"How?"

"Build a true haven—for everyone, including Altereds. We can preserve the future by letting go of the past. That's the goal we have, and every ally is welcome."

Wade considered the other man's words. It was a tremendous opportunity–and an enormous risk. By now, Vista Council would have broken the news about Estes Park to the population. He wasn't certain what the general reaction was, but he had a good idea. Disbelief first, then relief. Later, there would be questions about why The Vista had remained hidden for so long. Council would have carefully worded answers. Refugees had always been welcome, after a screening process while they remained isolated. Groups had seldom been more than a dozen people. An influx might lead to a logistical bog, but it wasn't an occurrence that could be ignored. When The Altered subject came to light, the response would be as varied as the people living there. He didn't believe it would become a point of conflict, as long as they stuck to the facts rather than fear.

"You have some influence in The Vista," Kaden said. "What about Cody?"

"I don't foresee a problem there, at least, not from the residents. We're still organizing the city. I can't speak for The Vista. We may be on our own because of what happened in Manitou, and that might be for the best."

Kaden nodded. "I wasn't suggesting you do this on your own. The Sixth have resources, too. I was under the impression people in Cody were hand-picked by you, and were aware of the subtle differences in your genetic makeup."

"Subtle differences," Wade mused. Shannon had yelled at him for using that word not too long ago. He wondered where she was for a moment. The next moment, he knew.

"That was interesting," Kaden remarked.

"What?" Chloe had seen him blink, nothing more.

"He just communicated with his partner in crime. Or, more accurately, his partner in the genetically enhanced."

Wade could deny it, but there was no point. He'd allowed the slip. Shan warned him that Kaden had picked up on her abilities. His concern, how easily that happened, and wanted to gauge Kaden's reaction. "She's been to Angelfire and gone east."

"Trade route," Kaden figured. "What's the problem?"

"Honestly? I'm a little jealous. I should have gone sooner and it might be me out there."

"What was stopping you?" Chloe asked.

"There were a few strays I wanted to track down," Wade said. "I wasn't up to dealing with Caulder. There are other things I'd like to keep hidden and they might have been obvious, because of circumstances out of my control. So I stayed close and did some hunting. Ended up in Skyline."

"What circumstances?" Kaden wondered.

"The offense didn't go like we'd planned; they never do. I took a double tap." Wade indicated high on the right side of his chest.

"What offense?" Chloe asked, thinking she'd missed an important part of the story.

Wade finished his meal, uncertain how to answer, of if he should bother.

"The only recent fighting we've heard about is..." She thought about it, certain she wasn't on the same subject as they were. "I mean, Rafe's compound got burned out a few months ago, right after the first of the year. Other than that, it's been quiet."

"Other than that," Kaden repeated.

"When did you get shot?" she asked.

"Right after the first of the year," Wade said. "Not too far north of here."

"And you're up riding around after, what, two months?"

"Three months. On cold days, it slows me down."

"A more common trait of our kind, about half of us heal fast," Kaden added.

"You were there, then," she said, surprised.

"Rumor has it," Wade told her, unwilling to disclose the details.

"I'm glad someone finally got him. Whatever happened, he deserved it." Chloe went back to her meal.

"You didn't hear it from me."

"What's the next step?" Kaden asked.

"Not immediately, but soon, there are plans in motion. Team Three has to meet and figure out what our next step is. The Sixth can be a part of that. You're my contact with the outside world. Shannon is working on Caulder, and our other partner, Mac, is working with Harlan."

"Caulder and Vance, as much as it looks like they're fast friends, aren't. That alliance has been shaky from the start," Chloe pointed out.

"Harlan Yates?" Kaden laughed. "This gets better by the minute. I've known him most of my life."

"I know," Wade said. "He convinced me I could trust you."

Chapter Ten

Kansas mid morning May 11

The rain was a steady drumbeat against the tent canvas, broken by an occasional growl of distant thunder. It was dark from the storm, the camp not bothering to attempt travel. Shannon curled up in her sleeping bag with a tattered old book. A solar disk heater hummed in the corner, keeping the room a pleasant temperature and giving her enough light to read by. Eventually, someone would come around and call her to go for a meal.

Almost as if on cue, as she began to doze off, there was a knock on the front post. Shan checked that her 9mm was next to her, under a blanket. "Yes?"

"It's me," Hunter announced, letting himself in.

"It's raining," she felt the need to point out, shaking herself awake.

"You don't say." He stripped off his rain gear, dropping them near the doorway.

"Why are you out in this? I'm fine here."

Hunter nodded, taking a seat. "I know, but I'm checking. I have a proposition for you."

Shan raised her eyebrows speculatively. "Let's hear this."

"The expedition Quartermaster has word there are flash floods all across the area. That's the main reason everyone is waiting until it passes. If the weather is better at dawn, he's sending people out to have a look at the roads. I thought, hey, who better to go scouting with than a Scout?"

"So we're going out in the mud and the cold, to see if the roads are washed out?" she checked the facts.

"If you want to. I thought I'd ask, because I get in trouble with you when I don't." He made a point of his previous mistake, and current attempt to remedy it.

"Daybreak?"

"Daybreak. I can meet you here."

"You can stay here."

"That would be fine," Hunter said. "If I didn't have a watch later. You're a guest, I'm not." He was the Councilor's son, but he'd asked to be included in the regular activities of the expedition. An already-trained security officer was welcomed.

"Great. Daybreak it is. We both already know there are washed out roads. It's a gimme."

Dawn happened, gray and dull, but the sky in the west was finally clearing.

"Slow down, Lt., we don't have to see the entire state today," Shan called, urging her horse to move along the trail faster. It was damp, not flooded or even muddy except in low-lying areas.

"You can call me Hunter," he said, waiting for her to catch up. It was a new place for both of them. She wanted to stop and look at everything, every rusted car, every abandoned house.

"Force-of-habit," she offered.

"Do I have to call you 'Captain'?"

She gave him an exaggerated glare. "No, you don't."

"It doesn't seem so important out here." They rode on.

"Are you quitting Vista Security?" she made conversation.

"Not quitting, officially or unofficially. It just seems pointless, because we're the only two Vistans here and I trust your judgment. Shannon."

"Hunter," she said. "I agree. I'll let you in on a secret."

"Last time you did that, we were looking for Wade up by Cody."

"I thought we were in Colorado, and you were riding us around in circles. I remember part of it. The parts when I wasn't so sick."

"You're on the job here. What's this big secret?"

Shannon looked around, back down the trail. The nearest riders would be over the ridge, behind them maybe a mile. "You knew our abilities were basically dormant."

"Were?" he caught the inflection.

"After we finished up in Manitou, after Wade and I got out of the hospital, things have become fluid. Especially for him, but I've noticed a shift, too."

He considered what that meant and realized he didn't have a clue. "I don't suppose you'd care to elaborate?"

She laughed. "The good news is, I still can't read your mind."

"How about anyone else?" He was only joking a little. They could spot a lie without trying, and knowing someone's state-of-mind was a simple thing, too, for them.

"No, it's not going to happen. The communication between the team is easier. We can be awake, no alcohol involved. I can pull up memories now, about thirty percent of the time I try."

"Ghosts." He was familiar with the reference. Ghosts of the past. "But Wade won't tell you what's happening with him."

"Same old mantra."

"No one knows everything," Hunter recited. He understood it now, after watching them hide what they were for the past year.

"I don't know if these are new abilities, or ones I've always had, that are evolving. Seeing ghosts is more complex, more complete."

"I've got one for you. Are there any Gen Ens here in the expedition?"

"I'm not willing to share that sort of information."

"I was aware, and knowing that, I can assume there aren't any."

"Any others," she nodded. "Angelfire might have a number of inactive Altered, but unless your father employed someone like me to observe the populace, he'd never know. I can't imagine he'd use one of us to find others."

"Politics wasn't the main topic of discussion. In fact, it was barely discussed at all. I haven't given up any of The Vista's secrets. Or yours."

"I didn't think you had. If your father, or anyone not close to an actual Altered, knows details about us, I'd be surprised. Vance said there were no fourteenth in the city. As far as I can tell, that means the Wildblood. They both must have a way of knowing who is who, and the only reasonable choice is another Altered."

Hunter nodded.

"He may be more aware than he lets on."

"I don't think so. JT didn't have specific information until you showed up in Colorado last spring."

"How did Vance know where we were? Because he did, he's said so more than once."

"Don't you have to meet someone to know if they're Altered?"

She nodded. "In the same vicinity. Say, a council meeting, a summer rendezvous bonfire, a winter solstice holiday gathering. That may not be true for every Altered."

"You've met everyone in The Vista?" he questioned, seeing how it was possible and wondering if she had.

"It took two years, to err on the side of caution. But yes. With Angelfire being two or three times the population, don't expect me to volunteer for that."

"The thought never crossed my mind," Hunter said, wondering if

Rafe had done exactly that for Vance. What worried him more, the thought that his father could have had dealing with the sociopath.

"Or Vance had someone in The Vista."

"That's a scary idea."

"Yeah. When are we supposed to rejoin the group?"

"When we want to eat, or when they stop for the afternoon."

She glanced sideways at him, skeptical. "You brought me out to the middle of Nowhere, Kansas, for what reason?"

"You're here because Command sent you. Has it occurred to you I might have a similar assignment?"

Still skeptical, Shan considered it. "You're not working for Command. I'm in Command, and I get a say on what Security does."

"You said Wade isn't talking to you," he emphasized the last word.

Shan got what he was implying. "Did he give specific orders before you left Estes Park?"

"He told me, if you ended up in Angelfire, I'd be responsible for your safety. It wasn't so much an order as stating the obvious. Because of where we'd be, not that you can't take care of yourself."

"Somehow, I'm not shocked." She wasn't angry, either. "Has Mac given you any orders?"

"Only that once."

"Good."

They stopped, the path cut by a wide gully. Hunter dug a flare gun out of his saddlebag and fired it in the air. "We've got a washout on the west side of the trail," he reported via radio. "Mile, mile and a quarter ahead."

The reply was a simple click to acknowledge. Then, "Scout on ahead to see how far the damage extends."

"Talkative," Shan said. "Let's follow the gully and see what's down the hill."

"Mud. Rocks, a few tree branches."

"Come on," she said, turning her horse downhill and heading off the trail. "When am I going to get a chance to sight-see in Kansas again?"

"Never, if you're lucky," he called out, following her. "I remember the Great Plains, from before the war," Hunter waved off towards the east. "Flew over them quite a bit as a kid. Running, after things went bad, too. My home is in the mountains. The flatlands are boring."

"That's good to know," Shan said. At the bottom of the hill, she kept heading west.

"I'm sure there's a collapsed barn, or something exciting, over here," he teased. There was a group of buildings, an abandoned farm, overgrown, rough, invisible from the trail. They rode on. "This far enough away from a city of any real size, I'd think it was the plague that got them."

"Or marauders. I remember, more than a few times, in The Vista. One of my earliest memories was hiding at the hospital. An inner room, with no windows. We'd sit and wait and it seemed like forever."

"Or they went some place safer," he suggested.

Dismounting, she walked a bit, getting a feel for the place. "I hope so." A small herd of mule deer moved away from their intrusion, disappearing down a long-forgotten driveway.

"I know what you're doing."

"Good. I expect nothing spectacular or complicated." He was there to watch her back, in case she got distracted by the tiniest details she might pick up, details that would go unnoticed by others.

"There's a lot of old farm equipment sitting here," he indicated along a fence line, half-concealed by underbrush and time.

Shan walked farther out, pulling away the weeds, wandering around it to get a better look.

"Do you plan on dragging it back to Montana?" Hunter asked. "For a souvenir?"

"I don't think this is farm equipment."

"So what? We need to head back soon." He followed her anyway.

Stripping as much debris away as she could, Shan stepped back and stared.

"Oh, Capt. Allen, now you've done it," he said, with a sudden and growing concern. "That is a fucking tank."

She nodded. "It's a tank that got hit by mortar."

"In Kansas." They both considered the implications. "Stranded soldiers, trying to get home. A tank could go places cars couldn't."

Grabbing her canteen, Shan climbed up on the carcass of the vehicle, scraping away dirt, revealing chipped and rusted desert camo paint.

"Here." Hunter pointed to the side below the broken turret, trying to clear the symbols painted on it.

Jumping down beside him, she watched while he uncovered markings.

"I'm not the history buff," he said.

She traced a red star on the side. "It's a Russian tank."

His mouth dropped open, like hers had a few moments earlier. "Are you sure?"

"Yeah, I am."

"Could this have been a movie set or something?"

"It could, I suppose," she said. "But it wasn't."

They were both silent again. A light rain started, with the sun still shining. "Let's see what the rest of these are," Hunter said, moving on to the next clump of buried machinery. In ten minutes, they discovered three more broken Russian tanks, lined up along the old farm road, pointed west.

"What should we do now?" Shan wondered, dusting the grime from her jeans.

"You're asking for my advice?" He was used to her having already decided. "What would Command want you to do?"

"Did your father give any indication of something like this?"

"Russian tanks in Kansas? The subject never came up."

"We need to get back to Angelfire. I have some questions and the assembly might have answers, or they might not. Hell, I might not even ask."

"I agree," Hunter said after a moment. "It could be risky."

"I'm in Security Command. That makes me as important as a Council Member."

"Are you going to tell them who you are?"

"Command, yes. Altered, no. This," she waved her hand at the war machines. "This has nothing to do with being Altered. It has to do with a flash flood, and our bad luck at finding them. I'm going to try one more thing before we head back to the expedition."

He was aware of what she meant and almost asked her if it was a safe thing to do. "I've got your back, just be careful. Take it slow."

Shan nodded, stripping off her gloves. "Direct contact helps, since I've gotten no substantial impressions by being here."

"Tell me if you see anything," he said, watching her grimace as she tested it, touching the star.

"It's cold."

Hunter kept quiet, letting her concentrate. She closed her eyes, humming softly to herself.

"It's October," she added after a few moments.

"What year?"

"You remember," she said.

He did. War Year, and Shan wouldn't be born for months. She walked down the path, still humming. "Don't wander too far," he warned, so she'd hear his voice.

"The farm was abandoned before the battle," Shan said, squinting in the bright light between rain showers. "And there was a battle, brief, one-sided. They were all running west, from the radiation, the war, and each other, no idea if there was a safe place to go." The ghosts, unclear to begin with, faded.

"Typical story, from that particular time."

"That wasn't as productive as I hoped," she said, rubbing her eyes. "It doesn't matter. I'll tell Mac as soon as I can. A Russian invasion is new information, even if it's twenty years old."

"What about Wade?"

"You said it-he's not talking to anyone. I can try, but it's more than likely not going to work."

"Try anyway," Hunter said. "If you think it's important or not. It might be the connected to the blackout in The Vista, four years ago."

"Good point. My report on the Blackout included an opinion that they were military personnel." She remembered the ghosts she'd glimpsed on the West Mesa.

"We should wait and not draw extra attention to ourselves. We'll be back in the city in a few days, maybe a week, if it keeps raining."

"You're being reasonable and cautious. It's scaring me a little," she teased.

"We're not running from Nomads, we're taking a pleasant trip back to Angelfire. You haven't seen the city yet. It'll impress you."

Shan nodded, knowing there was no real rush. The war had likely been over longer than she'd been alive. "Let's go pick JT's brain first and see if he's heard anything interesting. This isn't my first recent encounter with tanks."

Hunter didn't ask.

"It's May, Cmdr. MacKenzie. Summer is brief. We have a few things to discuss." Duncan spoke, Perro standing beside him, waiting for his turn. It was their usual approach.

"Are we doing this officially, or as officers having a chat?" Mac asked. Ballentyne was in the com room with him, and they both were aware of what the video conference was about.

"This is a formal request. Security Command is issuing orders to individual members of Cody Security and Team Three, to make yourselves available in The Vista for an inquest of the events beginning in September of last year and concluding in January of this year, in Colorado."

"Go ahead," Mac said.

"Lt. Taylor is present. Cmdr. MacKenzie, Cmdr. Wade, Capt. Allen, Capt. Green, Capt. Quinlen, and Lt. Hunter are all being recalled to The Vista, as well as any other officers involved. As members of Security Command, Team Three officers will be required to answer questions fielded by Vista Council after they are cleared by Command."

Mac and Ballentyne exchanged looks.

"Yes, that means what you think it means," Duncan told them. "Command is backing your actions, as far as Council and the public are concerned. It will be a closed meeting and the transcripts won't be available to the public."

"The rest of Command has read our reports. Are we under any sanctions?"

"As of right now, no," Perro stepped in. "There are some questions we'd like to discuss face-to-face. You understand, a formal request is an order."

"I am," Mac answered. They weren't saying anything he didn't expect. "You're aware, Cmdr. Wade and Capt. Allen are both in the field and out of contact. Officer Hunter is on leave, approved by me."

"On Command orders, yes. Hunter is a junior officer, so it won't be a concern, especially under the circumstances. Cmdr. Wade hasn't been in contact recently enough to for orders. Capt. Allen is checking in on schedule?"

"The schedule changed, but she's keeping with it."

"Recall them to Cody, Cmdr. MacKenzie, under a Command directive, the very next time you're in contact. Both of them. As soon as Team Three is together in Cody, you're ordered to report to Security Command." Perro made it official.

"By 'immediately', we mean within twenty-four hours, weather permitting. If there is a delay, you will contact us immediately," Duncan said.

Mac didn't get angry, even if there was a moment he thought he should. "Can we speak off the record?"

"Of course," Perro said.

"Off the record. Who would you like me to leave in charge of Cody in the middle of the summer?"

"Would you like us to assign someone?" Duncan asked.

"I'd like to understand why we're being treated like we've done something wrong."

"The time to discuss Team Three isn't now. Wait until you're here, because we don't expect any of you to be in The Vista over the winter, There are obligations you need to see to before then."

"Every member of my team is aware of their obligations," Mac said, getting short. They were pushing him, on purpose or not didn't matter.

"Remind them," Perro insisted.

"With all due respect, unless you plan on relieving me of my command here, don't try to determine how I should do my job from there. This isn't The Vista. Council and Command have seen that there's a status quo being maintained. We did what we were sent out here to do."

"No one is being relieved of anything."

"I may not hear from my team member for weeks. Months. We'll get to The Vista. It's our home. Were aware of those obligations. Stop reminding us."

Perro rubbed his eyes, and Duncan nodded. "You're children of The Vista, but not children anymore. Every one of you is a Security officer. Act like it. Get your team together, get to The Vista. It's important, Cmdr. MacKenzie. It's an order."

"What else?" Mac asked.

"Your request to open negotiations with officials from Black Hills has been tabled by Command," Perro said. "Don't take it personally and don't take it to mean no. All it means is that you need to be patient."

"We've been waiting," Mac said. "As long as I can remember. For next season, next summer, the next time it was convenient, or safe. The request was sent to you after contact had already been made. It was approved by both myself and Cmdr. Wade. The people from

Black Hills were here. We didn't have the time to wait for an answer."

"You don't have the authority to make that decision," Perro started.

"This is Cody. I absolutely do, and it's done. If you didn't want us doing the things we've discussed so many times, why did you send us out into the world?"

"You didn't give us a choice. There was an ultimatum thrown at us last summer, or did you forget?"

"We had a military-trained assassin hunting us. Every member of Team Three almost died in the past few months," Mac came back.

"We weren't aware of Cmdr. Wade being injured," Duncan pointed out.

"If he decides to include that in his reports. He's allowed to forgo private information," Ballentyne had an opinion finally.

"Being injured while on an operation doesn't count as 'private'," Duncan said.

"Except members of Command may make that determination," Perro corrected before either of the men in Cody could. "We've trained them well, too well, too independent of us. We've always allowed Team Three to do what they believe is best," he spoke to Duncan.

"And now it's coming back to bite us on the ass," Duncan said.

"I disagree. This is why they have to come in. Things that can't be explained from hundreds of miles away." He turned his attention back. "Cmdr. MacKenzie, there are facts you should have been made aware of years ago, and now we've waited too long. What you think is the truth may not be accurate, at least not as far as The Vista is concerned. We need to clear the air."

"I don't know if that's possible now, especially if Council is involved."

"Team Three being contentious yet again," Duncan remarked.

Mac didn't bother to respond.

"Get your team and get to The Vista. This is your final warning.

Charges will be filed by Command if you continue to ignore us. You have seventy-two hours to comply." Perro saw his opportunity to correct things slipping away. "Out."

"That could have gone better," Ballentyne decided, staring at the blank screen.

"Are you fucking kidding?" Mac asked. "They just fired me. You might be in charge of Cody in three days."

The wind shrieked through the narrow valley, rattling even the sturdiest of buildings as the storm set in. It had begun to snow as the expedition made it in, at nightfall, an hour earlier. Everyone headed for shelter, knowing it would clear in a few hours, or a few days.

"You might as well find something to do other than stare out the window," Hunter told her.

"This is like the storm when we flew in here," Shan replied.

He joined her at the front window, looking west up into the mountains. "At first, I thought you were joking about that."

"Not at all."

"You don't like to fly. I'll bet you like it even less now."

"We needed a hospital. Angelfire was our only shot. Otherwise, we'd have been out of fuel and on the ground not too far north of here. I don't know how long Chris would have lasted, in that."

"Good call."

"Lucky call, and some pretty brilliant flying. I'm going to recommend Green for a commendation when we get back to The Vista."

"That right there," Hunter said, "Brings up questions."

Shan tilted her head. "Oh?"

"Either Team Three is running the Cody Base their own way, or they're playing by Vista Security rules. Care to explain which it is?" He wandered back to the living room, closer to the fireplace. The condo was comfortably furnished, and self-contained. There was a stocked kitchen, bar, and even a library. Guests were rare, and well treated. Hunter had been staying in one of the duplexes since his arrival, despite the ongoing invitation to join his family in their neighborhood. Shan hadn't seen that. He thought she'd be impressed once she got the tour.

"It's a gray area, not either, or. We're working our way, what's best for Cody. Not a lot is different."

"And that's it? That's the truth?"

She nodded, joining him at the fire.

"How much trouble are you in?"

"Me, personally? I'm the junior officer of the team. I won't stand by and let Wade take all the blame. And yes, Wade is still AWOL. He's been ordered to report to Command, and he hasn't, not yet, not as far as I'm aware." Shan mulled it over, knowing he'd have more questions.

"Do you know where he is?"

"I know where he planned to be. It's no secret he wanted to go after The Sixth."

"Is he going to start a war with them?"

She cut a laugh off, knowing he saw no humor in the question. "No. As much as we were supposed to be super soldiers, or some damned thing like it, none of us want to start a war. Not with The Sixth, not with Angelfire."

"Not with Vance."

"Vance has his own agenda, and if Angelfire knows what it is, they're aware he's not the innocent bystander he paints himself to be."

"Rafe intended to kill you, for his own reasons."

"He'd have killed Wade and then me if I didn't fall in line. I was supposed to take Vance's place, when the time came, with restraints, of course. He'd never have trusted me."

"When?"

"This summer, maybe next summer. When he had the personnel. First The Vista, then The Sixth. The smaller villages would follow.

There would be no other choice. It was all very medieval, set in the twenty-first century." Shan said, warming up.

"All spoiled by a pissed off teenage girl."

"That's not quite how it played out. I wasn't alone."

"No way was I letting that happen, orders or not. Playing bait is dangerous, Shannon. You need to rethink your strategy."

"I'm not doing that now. I'm working on my own."

"Are you sure?" Hunter asked, seeing how she could still be a decoy. Distract the Angelfire Assembly while Wade was... whatever he was doing. If he'd stopped talking to her, there was a reason.

"I'm sure. I wouldn't lie to you about it. You're getting too good at reading me."

"You should be careful how you talk about the Gen En."

She sighed. "There's a better than good chance they know what Wade is. By association, I'm going to fall under suspicion, and JT thinks I shouldn't lie about it."

"I think you should."

Crossing her arms, she turned to face him. "Lie to your father? Am I in danger here?"

"No."

"I don't like the idea of lying. If it happens, I'm going to go with my instinct."

"That's exactly what you should do." He brushed her hair back. "I've had time to consider other complications."

"More? Fantastic."

"I meant you and I."

Shan hadn't expected the conversation to turn in that direction. "You don't owe me an explanation, Hunter. We're different, we're always going to be different, and the choices we make sometimes hurt."

"I was going to say, I've thought about it. A lot. I don't just give up and walk away."

She didn't understand, a brief shrug meaning he'd lost her. "You didn't have to stay here. The other side of the duplex is ten feet away."

"Not the point. When we were all back in Cody, I told Mac I wouldn't add complications to your life until we'd taken care of the problem. It surprised me when you showed up here unannounced. The point is, if you're willing, I'm willing. Let's see where this goes."

"Are we talking about sex?"

"I am."

"I smell like a wet horse."

Hunter chuckled. "We're snowed in for days, so relax. I didn't mean right now. How do you plan on getting back to Estes Park?" The grimace on her face told him she expected to be flying. "I can't say there's another choice, not unless you want to ride clear across Colorado."

"I'm not concerned about getting north, not yet." She caught his hand, entwining their fingers.

"We don't have to rush this," he whispered.

"We've been not rushing for a year. What's another day or two?"

"Yeah," he agreed, leaning in to kiss her. It was slow and easy, and when he drew back, he said, "You don't smell like a wet horse."

Shan smiled. "JT said someone would bring supper around. Let me know when. I'm going to find a book and go soak in the bathtub until then."

He had a clear image of that in his mind. It stayed there through dinner, a savory chicken and rice dish delivered as promised, along with a bottle of Pinot Noir. All the wine did was make Shan sleepy, and she excused herself.

The storm woke him early. Venturing across the hall to her room, he whispered, "Thunder snow."

"I heard," she offered, as he joined her beneath the heavy blankets.

"Haven't you been asleep? It's got to be three or four in the morning."

"Reading. I'm used to being awake all night. A couple hours down, and I'm good. What were you doing?"

"Talked on the radio a while, had a shower."

"I could tell," she whispered, getting close. "You got a haircut, sometime since you left the team. I was looking forward to grabbing a handful of that."

Hunter kissed her, more serious this time. "You don't have to talk dirty to me."

"No, you've got great hair, all wavy and blond. And that was a long way from dirty." She ran her fingers through the short stuff just above his ear. "I haven't had sex in a couple of months. You've been warned."

For a moment, he thought she was joking.

"A foot of snow, in April," Hunter mused, stomping his feet as they got to the lobby. It had mostly stopped, the haze burning off to gray skies, even at midday.

"It snowed in Cody last year, in July," Shan reminded him.

"I remember. You scared the hell out of me." She'd been injured, then sick, and he wasn't a doctor. "Nervous?"

"Not until you mentioned it."

He shook his head, amused. "Nothing to worry about, I swear. I'd give you fair warning."

"I believe you," Shan offered. "I'm never good at guessing how these things are going to go."

"Guessing? I've seen you and your cohorts stampede civilians and council members into doing what you want them to do."

Shan looked surprised at the accusation.

"Oh, don't give me that innocent look," Hunter said.

"That's not the case here. I'm representing Command. This is business."

Hunter nodded. "So are Vista Council meetings. I've got your back, either way."

JT had stopped near a set of double doors, waiting for them. Another man, clearly related to him, emerged from the assembly chambers as they approached. Shan knew she was in the company of all three Caulder brothers without asking. This Caulder, an Assembly member like his father.

"Capt. Allen, this is Phillip Caulder," JT introduced.

"Junior," she added.

"The Third, actually," Phillip said, extending his hand. "I'm named after our father and grandfather."

She smiled, a real one, not the facade she sometimes wore in public. Hunter had sealed files in The Vista. Learning something new about him made her feel like she knew him a little better. "Do you remember your grandfather?" she asked none of them in particular.

"Yes, and we can talk about our families later, if you'd like," Phillip answered, both his younger brothers nodding. "We're having a closed-door meeting, self-explanatory why."

They followed him inside, Hunter letting Shan go first and JT lagging behind. "One representative for every, what, five hundred people?" she wondered, knowing there were twenty-seven Assembly members and ten substitutes.

"Four twenty-five," Phillip said. "In the city proper. Outlying areas have their own representatives. There's nothing for you to be concerned about," he said, seeing her unease. "You're our guest. This meeting is the five of us, so the Senator can determine what is brought to the full Assembly."

"We've met, under less than ideal circumstances," Senator Caulder told her, inviting them all to sit at the table. They did, an assortment of beverages waiting. "Welcome to Angelfire, Capt. Allen. I'd like to say the weather has been unusual, but this is typical. I'll have some general questions for you once we've discussed the discovery in Kansas."

"The Vista has been isolated," Shan started, keeping it simple. "I'm not saying we've been without contact. The amount of information about the war and what's happened since has been limited. Everything is an unfamiliar experience for us, because of that isolation. I'm certain Chase has given you some insight into our situation," she nodded at Hunter.

"I'll tell you what I can, without dragging you into a history lesson that leads nowhere, because we've forgotten the question."

"My first concern. Was there a ground war here, in North America, twenty years ago?"

"As far as we're aware, no. That doesn't make it the absolute truth. We're under the impression you have information to challenge that."

Shan had video footage, and Hunter went to cue it up on the monitor they'd borrowed from the library room downstairs.

"We found military armored vehicles off the primary route. Russian tanks that had been disabled by artillery. We couldn't determine if they were hidden on purpose or by the passage of time." She watched as the video started, panning around the old farm, then stopping at the tanks. It zoomed in to show the markings and damage. "I didn't think it was a good idea to put that sort of information on the air."

"No, it wouldn't have been," Senator Caulder agreed. "Because of the lack of communications after the EMPs toppled the electrical grid, anything is possible. We've had intermittent problems in the eastern areas. That these intruders were military has been discussed."

"The Vista had an incursion a few years ago," Shan told them, deciding what she wanted to share.

"What sort of incursion?" the Senator asked.

"This was before Chase was in Security," she verified, knowing he'd be listening for details that might vary from what he'd been told. "A pair of military helicopters got close to The Vista. Security eventually took them down, without civilian casualties. No crew survived.

We suspected they were military personnel, but it was a single incident."

"There was an ICBM detonation reported in Montana, nine years after the war."

"Nine years after the war, I was nine," she pointed out, getting the distinct impression they'd set up questions to throw at her.

"You're twenty-one?"

"I'm twenty."

"And in Security Command?" Phillip questioned. "Do you have the ability to make these decisions?"

"I've been in Vista Security for two years," Hunter said. "I guarantee she has the authority."

"That makes her your boss," Phillip observed, eliciting a snicker from JT.

"The questions are for Capt. Allen," Senator Caulder said, knowing his sons and their teasing were all in fun. The questions were for him to set things straight in his own mind. He already knew the answers to most, but he wanted to hear her opinion.

"We were aware of the warhead," she answered. "It didn't pose a threat to us. I was nine, and yes, I saw it." Shan let it go at that. They couldn't find The Vista from the simple statement. Chances were, they had no way to pinpoint the location of the missile, aware only that there was a detonation.

"What do you want, here? Meaning, what is The Vista's intent with establishing contact?"

"The only family I have, everything I've ever known, is in The Vista. I'm here to see that it stays safe, and if necessary, isolated. I have the full authority to make decisions for Cody Security. Vista Council will make their own determination later this summer, but the safety of the city is the responsibility of Command. All parties are interested in establishing contact beyond what we have."

"The duty of the Assembly is to keep Angelfire safe. What is The Vista's stance on The Altered? JT tells me I don't need to explain the term to you."

"Command has strict rules about travelers, but none of those include monitoring people for being Altered. If there has been a political stance on the subject, it was before I was old enough to be concerned about such things." Shan didn't hesitate, didn't blink. Hunter ventured a glance at her. "Knowing what I do, I have to ask. Do you single them out, and if so, how do you locate them?"

"Until recently, we had a process of vetting The Altered. You put an end to it by killing Rafe."

Shannon snapped her gaze over to see if Hunter had known. He was as surprised as she was. She could see it, and more importantly, she could feel it. "You know what he was, what he was capable of."

"We'd always known about his sociopathic tendencies. We knew he targeted other Altered. Our understanding with him and Vance kept them away from our cities and territories. It was a guarded arrangement, for obvious reasons," the senator continued. "We were unaware of what the consequences could be. Your Team Three took a group of people to his stronghold and obliterated fifty or sixty of his soldiers. Vance told me the day after it happened."

"Good of him to share that sort of information," Shan answered, angry but not surprised.

"Important enough that I asked the questions, and he had answers. It's all classified, and he didn't name the people involved. When you contacted Cody and The Vista, the day you arrived here, your call-sign was 'Team Three, part one'. Would you care to elaborate on what happened in Manitou?"

"There's not much to tell, and no details I can share." Shan said, knowing neither Vance nor Caulder had figured out rid themselves of Rafe in a decade. "I have others to answer to. The information is not mine to share."

"You'd have never gotten that close, unless Wade was an Altered," Phillip reasoned.

"Are you asking me, or telling me? We had help from one of the clans led by The Sixth. They were selective in what they said, and they told us how to get to the camp, nothing else."

"That doesn't change the facts," Phillip said.

"It doesn't matter, not in The Vista, not in Security. Not to me. I was raised in the same home and I consider him my brother. If you want information about Wade, what he may or may not be, you'll need to talk to him, not me."

"You've suggested the general population is unaware."

"Council and Command are aware We're not going to change our stance, and if the decision was made to reveal these things to the population, it would be mutual."

"Even if they knew what The Altered are capable of? We believe Rafe, Vance, or both, were responsible for the warhead," Senator Caulder said.

"That's reaching a bit, don't you think, to put everyone in the same light because of what a few have done?"

"Is it?"

"You didn't get to be the leader of this place by dismissing allies as enemies or throwing veiled threats at them." Shannon paused, letting them absorb that. "I'm certain the governing bodies of The Vista know what The Altered are capable of. We don't need you. We don't need Estes Park." Not to mention, The Altered, the Gen Ens, were embedded in all aspects of The Vista. She didn't mention it. "We want to be part of the world again. That's why I'm here."

"It's good to have allies, Capt. Allen, but caution is the word. You understand," Senator Caulder agreed.

"We both understand that."

"The Vista cannot become recognized as a haven," Caulder stated. "Because of The Altered."

"We can be allies. It's a simple matter of semantics."

"When it comes to semantics in politics, nothing is simple," Phillip said.

"I understand that, too. What Command needs is your assurances that our people, all our people, will be safe here."

"I get the distinct feeling this isn't the first time you've managed your way through a council meeting," the senator observed.

Hunter crossed his arms, a smug sense of satisfaction.

"If we're done testing each other's boundaries, we can discuss details, or leave it to the councils," Shan said, knowing.

"Representatives of The Vista, Altered and otherwise, are welcome here. They won't be screened, or suffer any sanctions."

"I'll pass that along. They won't send any Altered. We respect your laws."

"Very good. On a separate note, I've been notified that your Command has sent word from Cody, to Estes Park, and now here. You are being recalled to The Vista. The word was 'immediately'."

"You have to go today, now?" Chloe questioned. Outside the stables, the sky had opened up, the deluge on its second day. It looked like the clouds were thinning, and perhaps the weather would break.

Wade kept packing his gear, a few weapons less because he planned on moving fast. "It's not my decision."

"You said you're out here on your own."

"And I am, but I still have people I'm responsible for. People I answer to. That's the way it is. Right now, it's time."

"I understand this is important, but I really wish you'd wait. An hour, Wade. Giles won't want to miss you, and he should be back." The pair hadn't developed a private relationship, despite being close in age. Wade with a debilitating lack of time, and Chloe confessed she was in a serious relationship. They worked together, and quite well.

"Not all day," he told her, giving in for the time being.

"He'll be here."

Forty minutes later, Giles and his crew found their way home, cold and tired, but uninjured. Raiders were burning homesteads east of the city. They were gone now, off to find easier targets as roads cleared of snow.

"You're leaving," he stated, pulling the saddle and blanket from his horse.

"The choice isn't mine anymore."

He nodded. "You told me. I didn't think you were exaggerating. For safety, do you need someone to travel with you?"

"No, I got here on my own, and I can get home. Besides, I move quieter and faster than you might expect."

"Will you be back?"

Wade resumed arranging his gear. "In time."

"A word of advice." Giles could see he already knew where this was going, and it didn't have a thing to do with being Altered. Wade developed an affinity for Skyline in the short time he was there. "Vance has been good for us. He's organized, gotten things back to where we can defend ourselves, protect our cities, keep trade moving. That doesn't mean he's perfect or even a decent person. It means he knows how to manipulate many people, for many reasons."

"Meaning what? Forgive his past indiscretions and move on?"

"When Vance does something, there will always be a payoff that benefits him. In the meantime, it benefits others. What you do is your business, and I won't say a word to interfere. Be careful, whatever it is."

"I will."

"We can't directly back you, not against him, not here. I know you've spoken with The Sixth. If you get a chance, tell them there is safe passage and shelter here, haven or not. I can do that, because I think Vance has far bigger concerns than infractions of minor statutes."

Wade didn't reply. They were waiting for him in The Vista. He'd be back, if he had Command behind him or not. He'd always have Team Three.

Chapter Eleven

"This all feels familiar," Green reminisced with Shannon while they waited. A lot of their time was spent waiting. "What did you think of Vance's pilot?" The barracks were as secure as any place that wasn't Station Two. They could talk, with a few precautions. He'd gotten orders not to leave her alone. For her safety, someone else, or an entirely different reason, it hadn't been mentioned when Mac spoke with him.

She held up an almost empty whiskey bottle. "Enough said?"

They came in late, one at a time, knowing Vance was aware and having them watched. Nine Vistans occupied the hotel. Mac had flown in a day earlier, Shannon and Hunter arrived by noon, and now they were waiting for Wade. Still, or again, however they wanted to consider it.

"Mac's going to see that, and after all the lecturing..." he started. They both understood Mac had a problem with controlling the amount of alcohol he consumed once he started. Shan didn't drink often, and that was a big part of the reason. "Did you steal that from the supplies downstairs?"

"Maybe, maybe not. Today is a free-for-all. Got booze? Drink up. Have some cannabis? Smoke away. Want to fool around, Capt. Green?"

"You're inebriated."

"A little. Not so much as you think, and not so much as I'd like to be. Tried it not long ago with Hunter and JT, and I enjoyed it way too much. When I get to The Vista, remind me I'm abstinent."

"Shan, you're abstinent," he offered.

"When we get home, not now. I'm working." She leaned on the nearest counter.

"You're looking for Wade."

She wrinkled her nose, her way of ignoring the obvious. "The sooner we can leave, the better. And also? Mac's asleep because he has to fly soon. So do you, so forget the invitation to smoke and drink."

"What's wrong?" Green took nothing she said lightly, especially if she'd been drinking. It made Gen En abilities easier to access. Or it had, before they'd gotten out in the world. All of their abilities were becoming easier for them now, except they hadn't been together as a team in months and didn't see it.

"I'll make you a list," she offered.

"What's wrong, right now?"

"I don't enjoy waiting. Not for Wade, and not to see if Vance has some nefarious plans cooked up for us."

"When will he be here?" He was relieved to hear she was aware of their current status.

"Minutes." She shrugged and had another drink from the bottle, grimacing.

He wondered if it was real, or a prop for Vance to have observed at some point earlier. Grabbing her hand holding the bottle, he pulled her forward a step and had a sniff. Whiskey. "Really?"

Shan cocked her head sideways. "Yes. Or maybe. Or just ask him. If he's not here by daylight, you're flying the first group out, so keep that in mind." She wandered off, interested in the food that had been brought in.

"Do you want me to follow her?" Chris Taylor asked, having arrived a few moments earlier.

"No, I'll handle it. Something's happening, and I can't tell what. She doesn't drink so much and that leads me right to thinking Team Three is about to set something in motion."

"I get it," Chris said.

"She said Wade is here. That means close." Green wasn't skeptical. If this was some plot against Vance, or if Vance was conspiring against them, he'd know soon enough. "Keep your eyes open, and if there's trouble, don't be shy about calling for backup."

"Maybe you should ask her what happened in Angelfire," Chris pointed out. "Hunter said she was drinking before they left."

"She doesn't like flying. Plus, I'm not in Command."

"Ask anyway. She trusts you."

Green wondered. The rookie seemed to have pretty clear insights, but then, Chris had grown up with them. He'd only been her second for years. "Whatever she's doing, it isn't my business. My business is to do what they tell me. The sooner you accept that, the less stress the team will give you."

"What if she needs help?"

"Trust me, you'll know, if it comes to that," Green said, dismissing him and following her to the kitchen. "Capt. Allen."

"Capt. Green," she acknowledged, rummaging.

"The alcohol is all out at the bar."

"I was looking for something to cut it with." She opened the refrigerator, peering in for a moment before giving up.

"Is there a chance you'll tell me what's going on?"

She shook her head. "When I can, I will. The only thing I have now is a bit of advice. When they start on us, step back."

"Meaning Command?"

"Council, Command, friends, foes, parents, strangers. Don't get involved, Damon, not if you value your career in Security."

"That's subtle."

"That word gets thrown around a lot, and I don't think anyone understands what it means."

"It's in the dictionary, as far from 'Team Three' as it can be," he told her.

"You can always retreat to the Ranchlands," she whispered, touching his face for a moment. "Do what I said, back away from it, and let us do what we have to. What's always been our plan."

"Are you handing out the same orders to everyone?"

"Everyone who's been to Colorado."

"This is going to be over and done with," he said, a little angry at her and a little angry at himself for letting it go so long without speaking his mind. "What are you going to do, then?"

"I'll drive circles around The Vista until it bores me and I retire to Dispatch."

"You're a little liar," he accused. "Not one of you could sit still long enough to let Command take the lead with Cody, and now you expect to go back to the way things were before? Not even for a second."

"We don't have a damned idea what we're doing next. We're going to throw a bunch of lies and half-truths at our bosses and hope we get away with it. That's why you need to keep pretending you don't know."

"Whatever you want."

"I want to go to Cody, dig in, and pretend nothing happened."

"They've already had preliminary reports."

"See there? All my plans, spoiled."

"Who are you flying out with?"

"Mac gets the rookie team, you get the rest of us."

"Hey," Chris popped around the corner. "Wade's here."

Shannon was pleased with herself.

"He said everyone should find a place to bivouac because we might not be leaving until noon."

"So much for sneaking out under the cover of night," she scoffed. "Vance will call for us as soon as he knows."

Green waited until Chris was out of earshot. "That's why you've been drinking. So the three of you can communicate while you're dealing with Vance."

"Or listening in if Vance will only talk to Wade."

"Why didn't you just tell me to shut up?"

She smiled. "I never get tired of being right."

"I understand you have a deadline to meet." Vance made small talk, with Wade this time. He'd been offline from Caulder a short while. Long enough to regroup and reconsider his options. Angelfire would offer asylum to the Vistans if the need arose. The idea left him wondering about his options with both parties.

"That's what I hear," Wade said. "I'd like permission for both flights to leave as soon as we have light."

"You have it."

Wade was cautious, sensing something new from Vance, something not at all pleasant. "You haven't been so eager to send us home. Why the change of heart?"

"I think my secrets are less interesting than yours. Let's talk about that for a moment, about being Altered."

"I'm not at liberty to discuss Gen En things." He called it by what he'd known it as most of his life. He didn't feel 'altered'.

"We both know that's a lie. The decision is yours, if Capt. Allen agrees with you or not. She's a bystander at the least, or a safe second opinion at most."

"Do you have a Sixth here, telling you these things? Because they're not as good as they claim to be, if you do."

"If I did," Vance agreed. "When I did, you waltzed right out to

Manitou and killed him. Rafe made certain everyone on the Front Range knew what would happen if we weren't here to keep them safe. He had his faults, and he was getting bored with this place."

"He was keeping them locked up in fear and the threat of retaliation. The arrangement, all along, and you wanted out because you were losing control of him."

"It doesn't matter. What matters is what people will believe. We've already had a number of incidents in outlying areas since word has spread that the stronghold was destroyed."

"I've been out there, and I'm aware of what's happening. As much as you'd like to think it's chaos, it's not. People are deciding the direction they want their lives to go, without the specter of Rafe following them." Wade had called it the moment he rode in to Skyline. There was a definite change in the air.

"When did you know you were a Sixth?" Vance crossed his arms, defensive not intimidated.

"I'd never heard the term until you told me, right here in this office, we couldn't trust them."

"You had to go find out for yourself."

"Yes, I did. I've spent too long trusting other people's word that there was nothing to see."

"When you found them, what happened?"

"We had a nice, long, and civil discussion."

Vance didn't believe it. "Caulder thinks you're a Sixth. He has reasons too, and one of those reasons is that Rafe told him all about you." The younger man had no visible response. "Capt. Allen didn't come up in the conversation. She might in the future."

"Capt. Allen can take care of herself."

"Does she know you're different?"

"It was a popular thing to label people," Wade said. "An Altered, a Sixth, a Wildblood." He was more adept at gauging Vance's reaction. There was surprise and alarm. "I understand what all those labels mean now."

"You should be more cautious about what labels you admit to."

"Just because you say I'm a Sixth doesn't make it true, and I've not admitted to a thing."

"The evidence certainly indicates so."

"If I am, it doesn't matter, not to me, my team, or friends."

"Are you certain about that?"

"Yes," Wade stated.

"I suppose you'll find out soon enough," Vance told him. "You have Cody, if nothing else."

It was meant to be a barb, but Wade ignored it. "I'll send word, as soon as we're on the ground, in Cody. Don't expect to know when we make The Vista. Their Council will direct any further contact."

"Good luck, Cmdr. Wade."

"Get them moving," Wade growled at Shan the moment she met him on the ground floor. It was hours before daylight, and the time was the least of his concerns.

"Green, Mac, standby for evac," she spoke into her radio, keeping pace with him. She'd been his bodyguard before she became a Scout, she knew his moods, and this wasn't the time for a joke. "What happened?"

"Vance. He's not obvious, but sooner or later, we're going to find out what his intent is. I don't think we're going to like the end results."

Shan nodded. "Mac has the rookies. We've got the rest of the original team. Green said we could be in the air, with ten minutes' notice. Are we going tonight?"

"Maybe," he said. "If either of us gets the urge."

"You already have the urge."

"If I still have it, in ten minutes, I'll make the call." They took the east stairs up, seeing no one. At this time of the night, it wasn't unusual.

"Trouble?" Mac was waiting for them.

"We're not taking the chance. Where is everyone?" Wade was past letting things be ignored.

"In their quarters, waiting for the word to go, or not. Everyone is on the floor and accounted for." Mac was out-of-character, quiet and serious. Like them, his abilities were changing. He knew they could be in trouble, a handful of them, a thousand miles from home.

"Call them to the rec room and I'll make the decision."

"Rec room, everyone," Shan gave more orders over the radio. They didn't believe the frequency was being monitored.

"You know what airplane and seating arrangements have been made," Wade cut to it. "Until Vista Council has solidified our position here, and in Angelfire, it's safer for everyone if we take ourselves out of Colorado and back to Cody."

"What happened?" Colin asked.

"Vance. I can't determine what he's telling Caulder, and I can't trust either at this point."

"So, we're out and Council will be the next contact?" Hunter wanted to know. He had obvious concerns.

"It looks that way. Your situation will get special consideration from Command, but that isn't a priority tonight. If you choose to remain here now, your position in Security will be terminated. I can't guarantee your safety with Vance, either."

"I wasn't asking to stay," Hunter told him.

"Good call, Lt.," Wade didn't let him continue. "When we get to the airfield, I've gotten clearance to go at daybreak. If that changes because we're going out early remains to be seen. Do not engage anyone unless I say it or do it first. Mac and the rookies go first and the rest of us will be next, five minutes behind. As usual, Capt. Allen is watching our backs. Our pilots have flown this route several times, so it shouldn't be an issue. Questions?"

No one had anything, or at least, that they were willing to bring up in the middle of an evac. "Great," Wade said, meaning it. "Let's go. Two vehicles, two airplanes, in Cody by mid-morning."

"Follow Wade's lead, follow mine, keep quiet, and if anything goes bad, keep your heads down," Mac translated.

Wade pointed at him, nodding. "Yes. Let's do this."

The drive up the mountain was uneventful. The guards ushered them in and let them pass without a word. They were in the air, heading east, then north well before daylight. It was a quiet flight. Most of the Vistans slept, while Team Three privately contemplated what came next. It had been nearly five months since their offensive on Manitou. In a few more days, they'd find out what the true consequences would be.

"Give me a couple minutes and I'll ride in with you," Green called to Shan, unlocking the storage compartments so someone could get their gear later.

They'd been on the ground a handful of minutes and scattered, too many things to get done and too little time before they headed to The Vista. Mac's flight had arrived at daybreak, nearly an hour before. He'd caught a tailwind. Now he had called a Security meeting.

Wade and Quinlen had gone out in front of the hangar to smoke cigarettes and discuss the next leg of their journey. Hunter, walking to town with a Guardian Team changing shifts, all of them looking forward to their first day out of Estes Park.

Shan leaned on the plane, wondering if she could manage to drive down the hillside without sliding off the road and wrecking. It had been months, and there was mud. The SUV parked out back for them was covered in it. There was a lot of work left to do in Cody. She contemplated spend the winter there helping out, maybe even driving circles around the place.

"Come on," Green said, motioning for her. "I'll buy you breakfast." He pushed the bay door closed and followed her.

"I accept. Wade said something about meeting with the Black

Hills people, so I'm on my own for now." They wandered out towards the parking lot, in no rush. Stopping, Shan asked, "What's that sound?"

A high-pitched whine, and since Green was shaking his head, she understood he didn't hear it. It wasn't a radio or a siren or anything she could identify. A moment later, it changed tone. He grabbed her because he did hear something.

Then the world lit up as bright as the sun. Like an...

Explosion, Shan thought. She suddenly found herself on the ground, trying to cover her head, Green shielding her. Blue sky shone through where the roof had been, and heavy black smoke billowing up. It was odd, there was no noise. She thought there should be noise.

Green was shouting at her, or something like it. His mouth was moving, but there was no sound. She wondered disjointedly what had happened to his voice. He struggled, getting to his knees, trying to get her moving.

"What happened?" she yelled back, the steady buzz in her ears making her own words sound distant.

He caught her face to get her attention and make her look at him. "Can you understand what I'm saying?" he asked, mouthing the words so she could read his lips.

"Yes," she nodded. It made her vision spin, equilibrium gone.

"The structure is unstable," he pointed at the gaping hole over them. "We have to get out."

"Where's Wade?" she asked. "Quinlen?"

He dragged her to her feet. "They were outside, in front." Staggering from the hangar, they made it across the road before he lost his balance in the gravel and they both fell down. "Stay put," he said after a few moments, then realized she couldn't hear him, hell, he couldn't hear himself. He pushed himself upright.

"What if they went back in, looking for us?" she pointed at the burning hangar, clumsily sitting up.

"They didn't. The other side is impassible." He didn't need to mention the building was engulfed in flames. There was a wide fire-break and it might not spread.

She shook her head, regretting it immediately. "Damnit," she said, hand over her left ear, closing her eyes against the waves of dizziness and nausea.

"Are you hurt?" he asked.

"I'm okay, but I feel like throwing up," she told him. The metallic ringing in her ears was the worst effect.

"That usually happens when someone tries to blow you up," he attempted a joke. The response was her putting her hands over her face, and he didn't know if she was laughing or crying. "Shan?" he touched her shoulder.

"I fucking hate airplanes," she announced, sniffing back tears, determined. "It's ugly to cry, too."

"Someone just tried to kill you," he said, serious this time. "You cry if you want."

Tucking her knees up to her chest, she wrapped her arms around her legs. "What do we do now?"

"We sit here and wait for the emergency crews to come pick us up." He figured she'd already tried to contact Wade. "Are they all right?"

"They're hiking around from the east. No one else was out here, because we were early getting in. Hours early." Shan thought about it, turning her head a bit to peer at him. "When you filed a flight plan with the airport manager in Estes Park," she said. "What did you list as our departure time?"

"6:30 AM. About an hour, hour and a half ago."

"So we'd be east of the Medicine Bow Range right about now, if we'd left on time." She sniffed, trying to dry her face.

He nodded. "A lot of open space to the east and Rocky Mountains to the west. With Flight One ahead of us, we'd have disappeared and no one would have ever known why." Green watched Shan and her expression never changed. "Do you think it was Vance?"

"I don't know," she admitted. "I can't think right now."

"If you imagine Wade was being unsociable before, this is going to set records."

"Yeah."

A four-wheel-drive jeep jostled up the road, the closest officers getting to the scene, no idea what had happened.

"Great," she wiped her face again. "Security Command doesn't cry and Team Three sure as hell doesn't." Fatigue, stress, and hormones had gotten the best of her this morning.

Green stripped off his leather jacket and wrapped it around her. "There, get it back to me when you're done with it."

Shan pulled it up around her face, wishing the day wasn't going be long and horrible. The same question Green had asked, was about to be asked by Security Command. Or at least Team Three.

"Medical cleared you," Wade told her. "Hiding in bed all day isn't going to make this go away. Come join us in the den." It wasn't an order, but it didn't have to be, because she knew he was right.

"Would it do me any good if I told you to piss off?" she asked anyway.

"It would not. It wouldn't offend me, either." He was in full Commander Wade mode.

"Then, piss off. I'm not interested in your meeting."

"I'll see you in ten minutes." With that, he turned and headed downstairs, leaving her alone in her room.

Shan huffed, flinging the quilt over her head, intending to go to sleep. It lasted two of those ten minutes before she climbed out of bed and began stomping around, looking for something to wear. Most of the clothes she'd brought from Estes Park had been in the Cessna.

"She'll be down," Wade said to the few Vistans called in for the briefing, joining them for a late breakfast. A late, somber breakfast, with the newest manifestation of his inner circle of trusted officers. Some of them weren't his choice.

"She was showing signs of shock," Green said. "Maybe we should wait."

"You're here," Wade responded.

"I'm certified Medical. I was there and agreed with Dr. Matisse. She's cleared," Hunter added. Letting her sit and stew was a poor option, in his opinion. It wasn't entirely a professional opinion.

"So am I," Green scoffed. "And I'd have said to call it a day. Fucking hell, if either of us had been a few seconds slower walking out, we'd both be dead."

"And she doesn't need to be up there by herself, thinking about it all day." Hunter crossed his arms and began to pace.

Green thought about saying something, then he thought better of it. They'd pulled some shrapnel out of his shoulder, stitched him up, and given him painkillers. Speaking his mind might not be the best idea. He turned his attention to the scrambled eggs and not-quite-burned bacon.

Mac cleared his throat. It was still his base, even after the threats from Command. He'd gotten his team moving, co-operating, and now this. "We'll get started now. If everyone's in as good a mood as Green and Hunter, we can always continue tomorrow. This shouldn't take much time."

Shannon stomped down the stairs, surveyed the room, and took a seat next to Ballentyne, at the end of the table, so she could get up and leave if she decided to. The right side of her face was red, like a sunburn. She'd slathered aloe on it, hoping to keep it from peeling. At least her hearing had nearly returned to normal.

"Want a plate?" Ballentyne asked, to be polite.

She declined.

"Do you want to take the lead on this?" Mac asked Wade.

"No, you're the one who has to write the report. Or not."

"First order of business," Mac announced. "Do we report this?" The people in the room – Team Three, Hunter, Green, Ballentyne, Lambert, and Elliott, all understood how clandestine the meeting was. Everyone in Cody was aware of what had happened. The official circumstances were about to be decided.

"We don't have an option," Wade spoke up. "Fifty-eight people can't keep a lie. Mishap at the refueling station."

"If we deny it's an aggression, what do we do to squelch the rumors?" Elliott asked.

"We don't. There are always rumors. Going out of our way with denial will make it look even more suspicious," Mac said.

"So we report an accident," Green said. "It's going to take a year to get another airplane ready to replace it. We're down to four, again."

"Again?" Shan asked, her mood improving with the company. She stole a piece of bacon from Ballentyne's plate and he winked at her.

"In February, Cody Flight Five snapped a support in the cold and damaged the wing. We started flying it again three weeks ago."

"Four airplanes," Mac repeated. "One burned in the hangar because of a leaking fuel tank and we're damned lucky our officers didn't get stranded coming in from Estes Park." No one had further comments about it. "Now, what in the hell really happened?"

"As far as we can tell, there was an explosive device planted in our gear," Wade started. "It almost certainly had to have been put there just before we left Estes Park or we'd have noticed it."

"Caulder has people in Estes Park," Green pointed out.

"Do you think he'd take a 50-50 chance of killing his own son?" Ballentyne asked, seeing Hunter flinch at the accusation.

"No," Shan said. "I trust Caulder far more than Vance, and yes, I'm being objective with my opinion. You know that."

"I agree," Wade said. "I reported to Vance that we were here and safe. He gave no indication of any deception during the conversation. It was a brief conversation, however."

"Maybe he told his people to arrange an accident for us, and doesn't know what, or when," Lambert thought.

"That's reaching to find someone to blame," Hunter said.

"Someone is to blame," Mac agreed. "Our short list is Vance and Caulder, in that order."

"What about The Sixth?" Green asked.

"There are a few dozen factions of The Sixth along the Front Range," Mac said. "Like any other established clans, they have differences of opinion. Right now, delegates from farther away are here in Cody, working on a trade route with us. We can rule out some factions, but not all of them." He'd learned a few things about those clans in the past weeks.

"Could this be Rafe's people looking for payback?" Lambert asked. He hadn't been there, as his responsibility had been in The Vista.

"No," Wade answered. "I watched him die. His people scattered."

~When was this?~ Shan asked him privately.

~When we went back and buried Noel and Parr.~

~Ghosts, then?~

~Yes. I'm learning to control that. So are you.~

"If we include all these factions," Mac said out loud to everyone. He was aware of Shan and Wade's exchange. "We're going to spend a lot of time mapping out who belongs where."

"Stick with the facts," Hunter agreed. "My father is interested in setting up an alliance, unlike Vance."

"Do you think he'd have told you he planned on killing your friends?" Ballentyne asked.

"He'd have found an excuse for me to stay in Angelfire." Hunter had it set in his own mind. No way was Angelfire was involved.

"I didn't get that impression from him, either," Shan added. "Vance wished he'd let Rafe kill us when we were children."

"Does it go clear to that?" Ballentyne asked, disturbed by the idea.

"Looks like it does," Wade confirmed. "Rafe was liberal with the information he gave us. He never feared us, even when he knew what we'd done. Vance, on the other hand, has secrets and lies hidden in everything he says."

"We left Estes Park off the schedule," Shan told them. "I can't prove a damned thing. As far as I'm concerned, it was Vance."

"I concur," Mac said.

They all looked at Wade, waiting for his opinion. "It might have been Vance. We can't work on assumptions, not here and not in The Vista." It seemed too obvious, too cut-and-dry.

"If Council sets up an alliance with Vance, are we going to be forced to work with someone who's trying to kill our people?" Lambert wanted to understand the situation.

"No, we won't," Mac said. "Council can supply their own security. No one in Cody has to run when they call."

"What do we do, then, about this incident?" Elliott asked, knowing he was on the outside of this group, a newcomer to Wade's circle, at Mac's request.

"We report the accident. It's not the first one concerning airplanes. It won't be the last," Mac figured. He'd been one of the original pilot trainees, back even before the rest of his team knew about the project to get air support for The Vista. "We go home and deal with that. We set up the treaties we decide on, as a group."

"There are few enough people here, right now, that everyone has a say," Ballentyne added. "Later, we'll form a Council and take votes, just like The Vista."

Shannon snorted a rude comment.

"Don't think it will change the way things are, Capt. Allen," he directed at her. "Security and Council will always be at odds. Here, and in The Vista."

"In Angelfire," Wade said, letting the idea float around the room for a few moments. "There's no reason to imagine, of all these factions and clans and cities, that we don't have allies and enemies right next to each other. We've been thinking too linear."

"When do we leave for The Vista?" Green ventured.

"You up to piloting today?" Mac asked him, and Green shaking his head that no, he was not. "Tomorrow after daylight."

"How about giving me one day without having to fly?" Shan spoke up. "I'm going to be pretty damned sore tomorrow from getting blown up today."

Mac sighed, and everyone in the room knew he was going to give in. "Day after tomorrow. Daybreak. Be there or you get to explain to Command why not."

"Who gets to conference call with The Vista?" Hunter asked, being the perky one in a room full of grouchy officers.

"I do," Ballentyne volunteered. "The rest of you need to," he shook his head, at a loss for words. "De-stress."

"Great. Are we dismissed?" Green asked.

"Yes," Mac said.

Green grabbed his jacket and headed out of the pod.

"I don't even want to know," Wade murmured. Team Three hung back as the others dispersed. "Don't expect attitudes to improve, not until we're home."

"I'm going to bed. I can't sleep when I'm flying, and I'm tired, among other afflictions." Shannon retreated, knowing they had private conversations to have. "I'll tell you about the tanks later."

"Tanks?" Wade repeated, after she'd gone.

"We should have that talk with Harlan," Mac said. "He knows more about it than Shan or Caulder. He was a witness to the war."

"Is it a good idea to leave her out of the loop?"

"She won't be. Harlan wants to meet her, and he likes to talk, but it has got to wait now."

"There are a couple of questions I'd rather she not hear."

"I've been stuck here, entertaining your guests," Mac reminded him. "But go ahead. I might have questions of my own."

"Have you two ever discussed your relationship and genetics?" The coffee was cold, and the group scattered. Wade went right to his concerns, knowing he wouldn't be offended. Neither would Shan, but he wanted to hear Mac's version first.

"A long time ago," Mac told him. "Before she became a Scout."

"After the Blackout?"

"Before that, before we started having sex. We had a good idea, even then, and we've been damned careful. That changes things, that changes everything, with both of us being Gen En. You said it – genetics. We can't take the chance."

"I'm sorry."

Mac brushed it off. "Don't be. It's not like we had any control over what they made us. We won't have kids together. It's not the end of the world."

Touchy subject, for more than one reason. Mac had fathered a child, back when he was a rookie in Security, long before Shannon. The woman had moved on westward with her clan, and he'd never even known if it was a boy or a girl. Thinking the subject was taboo was putting it mildly. Wade let it go.

"I wanted to wait until we got to The Vista, but with this airplane incident, someone is afraid of us and what we've learned since we left Montana."

"We've sure as hell stirred up something."

"Not necessarily what you've heard before. From the minute I met Vance, he was certain there were a number of Sixth in The Vista, and he's probably correct."

"How many are we?"

"I don't know because she won't disclose. At least some of those are The Sixth, as I've had it explained to me. We can argue all we want, but the facts are there."

"It's not just you," Mac realized, feeling the gist of the conversation change.

"I thought I was, after Manitou. Shannon did, too, and right now, as far as she's concerned, I still am. One hundred percent your decision to tell her, or not. My say in this doesn't matter."

Mac nodded. "Why me?"

"A lot of factors. Because of where you were born. The California Alliance produced more Sixth than any other entity in the western hemisphere. Because of when you were born, and because of your parents. We've known for a while that your abilities are about as different from ours as we are from the unaltered."

"I'd already decided, once I met Vance and realized his parents were Gen En, that his abilities were inherited rather than engineered."

"I didn't know about Vance," Wade confessed. "When he accused me of being a Sixth, I saw it."

"I told her we couldn't take the chance. I didn't tell her why, but she's not stupid. She knows we have inherited and engineered genetics."

"When you say 'we', that brings up another point."

Mac cursed, thought about it, and cursed some more. "I'd stuck to the idea she dodged that bullet."

"She did not. You've been pushing her towards Hunter for close to a year."

"We already suspected our abilities could be both. I didn't want her to be alone."

"That doesn't seem to be a problem. Are you going to tell her?"

"Damned if I know," Mac said. "Let's find out how brutal Command is on us before I drop more good news on her."

"She's liable to have figured it out already. Maybe not about the Sixth thing, but if she didn't see what Vance is, I'd be shocked."

"Do you think Caulder knows, and that's why he tolerates him?"

"Good question," Wade said. "Add it to the list of things the next 'Conda officer going to Angelfire can nose around and find out. Our first concern is what's waiting for us at home. Command has been keeping us from this all our lives. We deserve to understand why."

Chapter Twelve

The Vista mid morning May 26

The Cessnas touched down, five minutes apart at the airfield south of the city. Even with the impending hearings they faced, everyone was in a good mood. They were home, if there was hell to pay or not.

"This is outstanding," Shan declared, enjoying the first view of the valley she'd had in close to a year. The sky was clear, the mountain peaks bare of snow, with the scent of pine and sage on the breeze. The best spring day she could imagine.

"Yeah, we're out, standing in a field, waiting for a ride," Elliott joked. They had a laugh for a moment.

Half an hour later, they were standing in the second floor cafeteria at Station Two, where they'd been instructed to meet. Perro and Duncan were the usual pair that dealt directly with officers. Five more in Command were seated, some former Security and founding members of The Vista, in various positions security and civil for the past two decades.

"Team Three," Duncan said. "The rest of you, wait downstairs."

The members of Command, the ones that hadn't been off to parts unknown for the past months, had already arranged the seating in a semi-circle. There was no doubt it was an inquest.

"No quorum," Wade noted.

"This is unofficial, for any number of reasons we don't need to discuss for the time being. We have proxy votes and other members available, if the need arises." Perro had advocated for the team since their inception, a great deal of it without their knowledge. This was going to be painful for all concerned.

Anthony Haines, Council Chair Haines, made his way in and took a seat with the Command officers.

Mac had that 'we've-been-set-up' look on his face and both partners glanced at him, recognizing what he was thinking.

"You all know Council Chair Haines. If any of you have an issue with him sitting in on this briefing, speak up now."

"You said this is unofficial." Mac took the lead. "Just how unofficial?"

"No transcripts or records will be made of what is said here. The Council Chair has always had a vested interest in Command, the same as Command does with Council. He has sworn to not reveal or discuss in any manner, the information he learns here. You've been with Command long enough, you should have been aware of this," Duncan spoke to Wade.

"I was not."

"Right after the Blackout was the last time we had a closed conference, and Cmdr. Wade was Capt. Wade. He was also injured and in quarantine at Station Three," Perro reminded them.

"This meeting won't be be disclosed to other council members or any civilian," Duncan said. "Standard procedure."

"I have no issue with Chair Haines being here," Mac said, Wade and Shannon nodding in agreement.

"Where do you want to start?" Perro asked Team Three, giving them a chance to confess all, or beg forgiveness. He knew neither of those things would happen.

"Are we being prosecuted?" Wade asked.

"We're here to determine what actions come next. Have you committed any infractions, broken any laws?"

"No," Mac answered. "Not individually, not as a team. Can we at least hear a list of allegations?" His tone was the right amount of sarcastic to get his anger across.

"You may not. Command has spent years training you, instilling a trust we hoped you shared. That doesn't seem to be the case." Duncan was as angry. "We've been more than patient, and we also recognize it's as much our fault as yours. Team Three has been the star pupil of Security for years, and you've been spoiled."

"Time to deal with our problems," Perro said. "Your continued careers in Security are your choice. There are issues, first, and we're going to discuss them. Meaning, you're going to stand there and listen."

"Cmdr. Wade has been absent from duty since July fifteenth. Ten months, despite numerous orders to report to The Vista or Cody. Cmdr. MacKenzie, you left the Cody Base in early September with a team, to go look for Wade in Colorado, and lied to us for four months about where you were." Duncan paused. "Capt. Allen. Even after our discussion in August, after Command pleaded with you to trust us, you took off to Colorado without orders. That's just dusting the surface."

"As a team, you established contact with outside entities and started negotiating treaties, with no prior knowledge or consent from Command. That's a direct violation of our statutes concerning outsiders," Perro said. "You remained in Estes Park for an undetermined time. At some point, two of our officers were killed and Cmdr. Wade was injured in an incident that we still have no actual information about."

"There is no 'list of charges', because we wouldn't even know where to start," Duncan said, tag-teaming them with Perro. The others were sitting back to observe.

Mac caught it first. A moment later, both his partners understood.

"We're here to answer your questions," Wade told them.

"You've had ten months to come up with compelling answers. Every one of you is damned smart. I don't expect to be aware when you're lying and when you're not. But we do have questions." Perro crossed his arms. "We'd appreciate it if you would be truthful with us"

"Did they get a proper burial?" Duncan asked, not having to explain. Hearing a short gasp from Shannon, he added, "Capt. Allen?"

"They did," she offered, no details, no sarcasm.

"We told their families what the report from Cody said, that they'd been caught in a skirmish east of Estes Park. I hope we didn't lie to them."

"South," Mac corrected. "Big Thompson Canyon Road."

Duncan nodded, "I know. What were the circumstances of Cmdr. Wade's injuries?"

"Same incident, different location," Wade said. "We were in the wrong place, at the wrong time."

"You will check into the hospital here today, and get cleared by our doctors. So will any other officer that has been injured since you wandered off."

Wade acknowledged, sticking to the plan that the less they said, the better off they'd be.

It was Perro's turn. "You are Command officers, so asking if The Vista has been compromised isn't one of our concerns. We are concerned about Cody. Do you have unauthorized people at the base?"

"We have representatives from one of the nearby towns, and they've been consulting with us about what to expect, out in Wyoming." Mac figured he was still in charge of the base. They hadn't said otherwise, not yet.

"You just let them in?"

"We welcomed the advice, but no, we didn't just let them in. My officers and I met them before I invited them to the camp."

"Without a single word to Command," Duncan said.

"I didn't have the time to stop and ask."

"The team's standard excuse."

"What we've done was to protect The Vista," Wade said.

"I believe you," Duncan said. "It won't excuse our questions, or the consequences of your answers."

"This all began when Cmdr. Wade pursued the Nomads that ambushed Team Three at The Junction, on July fourteenth. The incident snowballed. Council caved to pressure from Command and granted them the Cody base. Over the next few months, Wade assembled a team of over fifty officers, all outside the boundaries of The Vista," Perro said. "A move meant, in part, to avoid an inquest, like we're having right now."

"We meant to take the fight away from The Vista," Wade said. It was the truth.

"If the fight had gotten here, we would deal with it like we have since the war. You remember the Blackout."

"We didn't want to involve more officers, or any civilians."

"That was never your decision," Duncan snapped.

"The people here are survivors, and any threat has always been dealt with. Yes, we have Security to contain those problems. We also have rules and regulations, so when things get out-of-hand, everyone, Security and civilians alike, knows what to do. You disregarded those rules. It doesn't matter what your intentions were," Perro spoke a lie. It did matter, more than anything else they'd learn today.

"Who decided to hide the fact there were other people, other cities out in the world?" Mac countered.

"A unanimous vote of the Council, right after the war, and then again five months after the bomb on Missouri Breaks. A delegation from Estes Park was sent out to contact us," Duncan told him. "Our choices were few, and none of them what we considered convenient. Those choices kept us safe and isolated."

"Then they already know where The Vista is," Shan surmised. Months of sneaking around the issue had been pointless.

"As far as being in western Montana. A Security Team picked them up. They were separated, blindfolded, and driven around in the mountains before they ended up at Station Three."

"Standard protocol," Mac said.

"It is, now," Duncan agreed. "Security in The Vista has gone through changes to keep up with additional problems. You're all too young to remember what it was like before the warhead. When I say things have changed, I'm not being flippant. Security now is nothing like what existed in the beginning."

"Next question," Perro continued. "Have you made any commitments in the name of Command or The Vista? Yes or no?"

"No," Shan answered as he looked at her.

Then Wade. "No."

"No," Mac said.

"When did you plan to return to The Vista?" Duncan didn't direct the question at any of them in particular.

"Being in command of the Cody Base, I had no plans," Mac said. "Except for new orders."

"At the end of the season," Shan spoke up when it was clear Wade was contemplating an answer. "Angelfire has a wealth of knowledge, pre-war and otherwise, but I wanted to be in The Vista or Cody for the winter."

They waited for his answer.

"Wade?" Shan urged.

"I had no plans," he announced. "No plans to get to Cody, no plans to make my way back to The Vista this year. I've learned more out there, in the past five months, than I have here for the past decade." They asked for the truth, and he obliged.

"You think that's reason enough to ignore your orders?" Duncan asked. "It had to occur to you, working under Command directives was void after about a week."

"My options were fluid, something Command encouraged Team Three to do in any situation. I didn't have a direct order until Mac contacted me a week ago." He was defensive, arms crossed, feet planted, knees locked.

Perro rubbed his eyes while Duncan sat back in his seat, frustrated.

"Tell them," Haines said.

"We needed five more years," Duncan said, sullen, contemplating what might have been.

"In five more years, we'd have lost them. We damned near have right now."

"Five more years for what?" Mac asked what all three were thinking.

"Five more years, because a thirty-year-old is far more prone to reason and logic than a twenty-year-old," Perro said, meaning them. "We spoke with you, weeks ago and said there were issues we needed to discuss face to face. Because you are Team Three, you've had suspicions, years' worth of them, I expect."

"We've had ideas about a lot of things, most of them out of our control," Wade said. "You're going to need to be more specific."

"Oh, we will. While you say everything you've done was to protect The Vista, we don't doubt you. We hoped this could wait, but Haines is right. You understand what we're going to tell you was all done to protect The Vista as well. And you," Duncan sounded cryptic.

"When we came to The Vista, and began comparing the circumstances of our lives, it became more apparent," Haines spoke up. "Too many coincidences to be random."

"What you are isn't a secret to us," Perro told them. "We're aware, we have been since the beginning. It's that simple. We've known since those first months after the war, that some of our children were different for a reason. Twenty years ago, there was more evidence of it. Council, and later Command, has gone about meticulously removing traces of our past that might threaten our children, and their future."

"That's the reason for the isolation." Mac was surprised by the revelation. None of them had seen it, even if they suspected.

"One of many."

"I remember the radio transmissions, searching for other survivors," Shannon said, heading towards a question. "Were those real?"

"Yes, of course," Perro said. "We wanted to find others. You don't always get what you want. When that failed, we had to find ways to protect ourselves against what might be out there. Your schooling was exhaustive, but Cmdr. MacKenzie gravitated towards Security without our influence. You two followed, and all of you soaked up any information we provided. They made you strong and smart. We kept you safe, and in the shadows. It took them damned near twenty years to find you, which was far more time than we expected. We got lucky."

"Nine years," Shan corrected. "That bomb on Missouri Breaks was a warning."

"Yes," Perro agreed. "To us. We had no way of stopping others from gauging your reaction. We had an understanding with Vance. He held up his end of the agreement for a decade."

"What are we, in reality?" Wade asked.

"We've watched you piece it together for years, despite our caution. The three of you are genetically enhanced, but you are as human as the rest of us. Never let anyone tell you otherwise. Now that you've ventured out beyond The Vista, it will happen," Perro assured them. "The information we have will be made available to you. I'll warn you, it's not going to answer your questions."

"You called it 'Gen En' when I was barely old enough to understand what you were talking about," Shan spoke to Wade. "You weren't wrong."

"What others?" Mac asked, going back to something Perro said.

"Estes Park was the first. We discovered places, smaller and less organized, over time. We were aware of Angelfire, with little else to go on," Perro said.

"All we knew for certain was that we had to protect you until you were old enough to understand, old enough to protect yourselves," Duncan told them. "We misjudged."

The room went silent, too many implications to be voiced.

"It doesn't excuse you from the reason we're here," Perro said.

"No," Mac agreed. "We didn't think it would. All this time, while you mislead everyone else, you were misleading us by default."

"Not by default," Perro confessed. "We never meant for you to be told unless it became unavoidable. Until last July, nothing about the situation was clear to us."

"How many people are aware?" Wade asked.

"Not as many as you're imagining. Between two and three dozen," Perro told them. "Various members of Command, Council leaders over the years."

"Our parents?" Shan asked.

"Not unless they've kept it to themselves all this time, with the one obvious exception."

The exception was his mother, and Wade ignored the unspoken accusation. She worked for a biotech before she discovered what they were doing in their secret labs. "What do you want from us?"

"We want a comprehensive list of who you've been in contact with, what you've told them, and what to expect over the next year from them. Capt. Allen, we require a detailed report on Angelfire. Cmdr. MacKenzie, same for your guests in Cody."

"What if we can't do that?" Mac asked.

"Do you want to remain in Security? In Command?"

"Yes."

"Find a way," Perro said.

"I've got nothing about Angelfire to hide," Shan offered.

"Good," Wade said. "That makes one of us."

"Are you refusing the order?" Duncan asked.

"I'm stating the fact that I won't endanger the lives of anyone, here or otherwise, by revealing where I've been or who I've contacted. You don't understand the realities about life outside The Vista, so you can't give me an order like that."

"I just did. Perhaps you can take the time to explain the world to us."

Wade shook his head. "Would it matter?"

"Cmdr. MacKenzie, are you going to give us a report?"

"I'd like to confer with my guests in Cody before I make that decision."

"Team Three, would you step into the foyer while Command discuss these issues," Perro said, an order rather than a question.

"Are we fired?" Shan asked the moment the door closed. "Because we're in Command, too. Doesn't kicking us out take a vote of the full membership?"

"We're in Command," Wade reassured her. "And if they fired all three of us, what difference do you think it would make?"

"They'd put someone else in charge of Cody."

"Who? Not anyone in the 'Conda. So, Duncan? Someone else? That's not going to happen, and again, even if they did, so what? We can take our officers and set up in Casper before snowfall."

"Two hundred miles," Mac contemplated. "We could do it, if we're willing to sever those ties. I don't think we are. I think they know that."

"I didn't know," Wade answered their unasked question. "They had enough insight to keep us in the dark this long. One of us should have figured it out. We didn't. Now we'll pay the price for it."

"Does this change anything?" Mac asked.

"No, not a bit. We go with what we decided."

"It didn't look that way to me," Shan added. "You're pushing them."

"If I let it go easily, they'd wonder why."

"He has a point," Mac agreed.

"I don't like it," Shan said.

"You've already told us a dozen times." Wade shrugged. "Whatever they decide, it's beyond our control now. I won't be responsible for giving people up to Vance, and that's exactly what it would amount to."

"I've set up a trade route with Black Hills. If we have to move south, it could delay progress. I don't think it will stop it. Wade's right–Vance would retaliate against the villages in his territory. Black Hills is out of his reach, and Harlan isn't afraid of him," Mac added for clarity.

"We might need that alliance more than ever," Shan said. They fell silent again, waiting to be called back, to find out if they were a team, if they had jobs. The wait was brief.

Perro ushered them back into the makeshift office. "Your Command positions are not in question. Should any of you choose to resign, there will be no inquiry. However, we're going to discuss your Security positions."

"Specifically," Duncan went on. "Capt. Allen, you are the junior officer of the team. While we believe you acted in the best interests of The Vista, and under orders from other team members, we also can see your influence in the team is every bit as strong as theirs. This is a formal reprimand, one that will be permanent in your files. It includes a step down in rank. We expect full cooperation concerning Angelfire, or the reprimand will include further loss of rank, to begin with. Do you understand?"

"Yes, sir," Shan said.

"Cmdr. MacKenzie," Perro went next. "At this time, we have no choice but to trust your judgment on the outlanders issue. We don't want to endanger possible alliances. You are ordered to file reports with us daily upon your return to Cody until the issue is resolved to the satisfaction of Command. There will be further orders, as needed. This is a formal reprimand as well, permanent in your files, and so on. We don't want to replace you, but we have the means to do so. Do you understand these orders?"

"I understand."

"Cmdr. Wade," Perro continued. "You disregarded orders over most of the year. We also understand your wish not to involve civilians that may be in danger if their connection to you was discovered. Again, that doesn't excuse your actions."

"His job is to protect civilians. Nothing limits that to The Vista, or Montana," Mac pointed out.

"We're not judging his intent, but his methods," Perro said.

"Maybe it would be better to excuse the rest of the team," Duncan suggested.

"We're a team," Shan protested. "We have a right to hear what Command is doing."

"It wasn't a request," Duncan said.

"I don't care. This isn't right."

"One minute," Wade told them, grabbing her by the forearm and leading her to the back of the room. Mac stood there, regarding the Command officers.

"This is bullshit. It's as much of an ambush as what happened at The Junction in July," she whispered to him.

"Take a breath," Wade directed. "Look at me." She did, and he released his grip on her arm. "We've been over this. It's going to happen if you get yourself in more trouble or not. I know you're embellishing, and you can get caught up in it. Don't. Step out in the hall so we can get on with this."

"I got it," she said, taking a deep breath.

"Do you trust me?"

"Of course."

"Then do what we decided was for the best. Let go, Shan, it's just a name. We'll be a team if that's what they call us or not."

She nodded.

"Remember that you're a Security Command officer."

"I can do that."

They walked back together and joined Mac.

"Cmdr. MacKenzie, Capt. Allen, would you wait downstairs until we call for you?" Perro asked. "You understand non-disclosure."

Shannon bit her tongue and didn't point out to Perro that he'd just busted her back to a lieutenant. They did as they were asked, taking the stairs. The lobby was crowded with officers, some waiting for their turn with Command, and others for moral support. Both Taylors were there, Green, Hunter, Elliott, and the younger MacKenzie. More, too, but they were the ones that had to be there. Later, the entire group would be released from the briefings.

"Can you tell us anything?" Lambert asked, seeing them first.

"We can't," Mac said. "We're almost finished."

"Finished upstairs, or, you know, finished?"

Mac raised his eyebrows. "Yeah, that."

"Which?" Lambert and everyone else in the room were waiting for the answer.

"I think it's a coin toss."

"We can stage a sit-in, or a sick-out. Something," Lambert offered.

"Don't blame Command," Mac told him. "We did this, and we understood what the consequences would be. Security is Security and we do our jobs. Otherwise, this would all be pointless."

Chapter Thirteen

"Cmdr. Wade, we cannot simply look away from what you've done, and failed to do, over the past months," Duncan spoke for the group, but not Command, not officially.

"I never expected you would." Wade was blunt, as always. They'd suspect everything since July was fabricated otherwise.

"No, you didn't. As careful as we tried to be, we should've been more honest with you, with all three of you."

Downstairs, Shan leaned over to whisper to Mac. "They don't know."

"Why The Sixth were created," Mac said. In short, to survive the end of civilization. It hadn't worked out as planned.

"We need to tell them."

"Or maybe we don't. What's the point, twenty years after the fact?"

"We're asking you, off the record, to resign your position in Security," Duncan went on. It hurt, too. He'd trained all three of them at some point. Wade had been the most serious, and now this.

"You didn't need to ask." Wade produced folded papers from his jacket. "My resignation, five copies worth. If you want the same of my Command position, it's yours."

Duncan hesitated. "That was never our intent."

"It should be. If I was looking at this, about another officer in Command, I'd call the vote. I have my reasons. I can't tell you most of them. What I will say is that if we had known, it wouldn't have stopped the Nomad, the one called Rafe, from what he did. He was trained with his engineered abilities, a luxury we haven't had until now. That's why I'm doing this. The only way to ensure someone like him doesn't come after us again is for us to scatter. Together, others see us as a danger. Together, we're a liability."

"We can guard against it," Duncan started.

"It wouldn't matter, not now. Maybe in time. The Vista is important, more than the fact that we're here, but because we're strong, we have been out of the reach of Vance and others like him. They've been forced into compromises to survive. We don't need them."

"What do you suggest?" Perro asked.

"Accept my resignations. I don't care what you put in the reports, but my family and my team will. Send out your delegates. Don't trust Vance. Let us do what you've trained us to do."

"You want to do this without the support of Command," Perro said.

"It releases Security of any perceived involvement."

"But you want Cody to be in the control of your core group of officers," Duncan pointed out.

"They already are, and I can't see Command wanting to change that. We've made progress. Don't let my actions blind you to that."

"You've all taken liberties with your Command positions. We'll accept your resignations, as we can't ignore the facts. Because Cmdr. MacKenzie is in charge of Cody, and Lt. Allen is a Scout, Team Three will be disbanded."

"They don't need the reprimands on their records."

"I doubt they care. The reprimands stay, as do the conditions of their continued duty in Security. You've led them to this, Cmdr. Wade. Keep that in mind, for the future."

"You just told them we were equally to blame."

"If you hadn't started this rebellion, of sorts, there wouldn't be an issue. They followed your lead."

"If you think for a second I led them astray, you don't know us at all."

"I do know you, Wade, and them. They'd follow you anywhere, they'd do anything you asked. Tell me there's never been a time you've crossed the line. Tell me they didn't stand there with you."

"No," Wade denied. "This year has been a whole new foray for us."

"I wasn't trying to get you to incriminate yourself," Duncan said. "I think we're finished here."

Wade handed him the bundle of papers, turned on his heels and headed downstairs without another word.

The silence was brief. "Have we lost them?" Locke asked from the sidelines.

"It feels that way, doesn't it?" Perro thought out loud. "I don't know. After their anger cools, they'll understand why."

"As hot-headed as Allen and MacKenzie are, Wade holds a silent grudge. Then later," Duncan shrugged. "There could be hell to pay if he takes it personally."

"Do you think he did?" Locke wondered.

"I don't. He understands it's Command business. If it was personal, he wouldn't have just walked away."

"We ended his career on technicalities. He walked away for his team," Perro told them. "Don't forget it. We may lose a lot more than Team Three over this. The 'Conda owns Cody, and they know it."

Hours later, after the rest of the hearings, after a Station-wide debriefing, after a slew of family reunions and a picnic get-together in the park across the street, Mac tracked Shannon down. The sun was beginning to set. She'd found a table under a massive elm tree and waited for him, watching the crowd. Eventually, they'd disperse, wandering home well after dark. This was The Vista, and it was a safe place again.

"Hey, stranger," he greeted, holding her for a long time.

"That could have gone better."

"That played out almost to the letter of how we decided it would."

"Almost," she agreed. "Still could have gone better. We should've held our ground."

"For what? We've got what we wanted. Cody is ours."

Again, she had to agree. "You sound like Wade. They lied to us, to protect us. We lied to them, to protect them."

"You're angry they could do it all these years, and we were the clueless children, just like they wanted us to be." He wasn't angry. Surprised. Even a little impressed. As for Team Three, they'd believed they had cornered the market on subterfuge.

"When are you going back to Cody?"

"No idea. Right now, I'm supposed to convince you to do some Command business. They want to have a discussion about tanks."

"Great." She didn't know it would be so soon. It was important, though. Perhaps not as urgent as she'd thought a few days after the discovery, but it needed to be addressed. "Hunter was there."

"Taylor's looking for him. Wade and Duncan are waiting. You talk to them, you talk to Command as soon as they call everyone in. Maybe tonight, but considering the war has been over for a while, they might wait until tomorrow. Might."

"That's what I was thinking," she agreed, hopping off the table to walk with him. "What did he tell you?"

"Hunter? Not a thing about tanks. Another reason I need you in Cody. Harlan told me what happened because he was a witness to the war. Then he showed me."

"Ghosts?" she was intrigued, twining their arms as they walked towards the station.

"Better. Videos, ones they managed to salvage. Interesting stuff. I want your opinion, Wade's too, but I don't know if that will happen."

"So, was there a ground war here, in the west?"

"Not this far north. Short answer is yes. Russian forces invaded Texas a few weeks before you were born. There wasn't a Russia by then, or any other country, but they needed a new home in a more temperate zone. Texas got hit hard by the virus and had no defenses left. One plus one equals two. Invaded isn't accurate, either. An occupation."

"Shit."

"That's what I said. It probably makes the Blackout a military incursion."

"Are we going to discuss that with Command?"

"Bring it up," he told her. "You can still do that, Lt. Allen."

"Shut up," she answered. "Harlan. Yates?"

"Yes."

"I'm impressed."

"Don't be. He found Wade and headed him in the right direction to look for The Sixth. Wade sent him to Cody, in case the clans around Wyoming didn't want new neighbors. Not all the Sixth are as friendly as Kaden, apparently."

"I didn't say Kaden was friendly. I said he didn't want to kill me. Not the same thing, by the way."

"Good point." Mac waved at a group of rookies heading out to patrol the park and downtown. He remembered that duty. Seven years. It didn't seem that long ago. "Worried?" he asked, holding the station door open.

"No, I'm not. I wasn't earlier. This, though, this is what we went out there for. To find out what's been happening in the rest of the world."

"Or points within our range."

"Sure." Shan stopped, contemplating something non sequitur. "We're all right, aren't we?" She didn't have to explain.

"Of course," he said. "Did you think we weren't?"

"No. I like to hear it."

Mac pulled her close again and whispered as a handful of Command officers made their way in from the opposite doorway. Wade and Duncan were there, too, with people gathering for the next briefing.

"I don't want to forget how you feel," she told him. It wasn't just a physical thing, and they both understood.

"It won't happen. I'll remember how you feel, forever. It has nothing to do with what we are, but everything to do with who we are." He lowered his voice, speaking for a few intense moments, letting her go after those moments passed. He'd said what he needed to say.

"That's going to make some great rumors," she observed. "At least, I hope it does."

"Oh, Shan, they already know. If they've always known everything else about us, they figured that out a long time ago."

She smiled at him. "Let's get this over with."

It was Mac's turn to be pessimistic. "This is going to go on all night. We have ten months to catch up on."

"Stop trying to cheer me up," she said, faking distress.

"Either get in here, or go home," Duncan called across the hall. They made their way over, knowing it wasn't a choice. "Tell us about your tanks, Lt. Allen," he invited.

***

"You wouldn't still be here, if there wasn't more to the story," Perro said.

It was unquestionably late, or ridiculously early. After the discussion about tanks ran its course, Mac had gone home. He was scheduled for another Command meeting at 9am, less than six hours away.

Hunter and Shan engaged in a deep discussion about who was driving where. She prevailed, and they'd went off to her parents rather than Station One, clear out at Anaconda.

Duncan excused himself, but returned a few minutes later, bottle in one hand and three glasses in the other. Wade sat back, waiting to see where this was going.

"You didn't have to resign," Duncan repeated his stance from earlier in the day. He passed the glasses and added a decent amount of amber-colored liquid. "Bourbon," he noted, taste-testing. "The good stuff."

"I did," Wade said, stating the facts as he saw them. "It distances me from Command, and from The Vista. If the time comes, when you have to claim I've gone renegade, it will make it seem more plausible."

"Why now?" Perro asked.

"The tanks were our first concern until someone tried to end us. I don't mean last year."

"Another incident unreported?"

"This has to be off the record."

"Then it is," Perro told him.

"The accident at the fueling depot."

"Could you be more specific?" Duncan asked.

"I might not be here now if I had the answers," Wade contemplated what he wanted to do, after the initial anger had passed. "There was no accident at the airfield two mornings ago. There was an explosive device on Cody Flight Two. If we'd departed when we were supposed to, when the flight plans showed, we'd have been about an hour out of Estes Park. As it was, we were on the ground a few minutes."

"What are you going to do?" Duncan asked.

"What I have to."

"That's what Command is afraid of," Perro pointed out.

"There are things we can't control," Wade explained. "One of those things is that there are Gen Ens who are able to sense others."

"We suspected something like that."

"Thought it was possible," Duncan corrected. "We had the information and as you got older, it seemed plausible to us. We've never been in a position to understand, not without giving away the fact that we knew, or that we were protecting you."

"The thing you should understand is that I resigned so you don't need to ask those questions. I'm going to Colorado before winter. My first responsibility is to The Vista, and that's why I'll go. Shannon and I, when we're together, are like a catalyst for each other. It makes it easier for those Gen Ens to sense us. I'm not making anything easy for them."

"Do you know who planted the bomb on your flight?"

"I have my own ideas about it, ones I haven't shared with my team." They might tell him there was no Team Three now, but that was their opinion, nothing more.

"Would you care to share them with us?" Perro asked.

Wade considered it. "No, not unless this conversation is strictly between the three of us. If other Security officers would hear, they might think they could retaliate, and they can't."

"It doesn't leave this room," Perro said.

"You don't repeat it to anyone, even in this room," Wade said.

Duncan laughed. Wade tended to be too literal. "We won't repeat a word."

"I mean it, and I mean you can't let this influence your Command decisions."

Both older men nodded, intrigued.

"I'm more than certain it was Vance. I just can't prove it, and right now, there is a tiny amount of doubt."

"That's good enough for me," Duncan said.

"But you are aware of none of this," Wade said. "When I lose that doubt, I'll decide what I'm going to do."

"If anything," Perro added.

"Agreed," Wade said. "If I decide to do anything. That might not be an option. Vance kept Rafe under control for years, or so he claims. I have suspicions about that, too. In the beginning, I suspect Vance kept him from hunting us. That ended at about the time of the bomb on Missouri Breaks."

"That makes him dangerous."

"He's the governor of Colorado, or the post-war version. He created the position by force and he kept a hold by fear. The fear that Rafe would be on the rampage if Vance wasn't there to stop him. I think that's a lie, fabricated by the two of them, or maybe more, to do what has happened. Vance has control over almost half the trade routes."

"Where does Angelfire figure in this?"

"Caulder came out of nowhere, and Vance dealt with him as best he could. There were other internal problems, and Cmdr. MacKenzie has an insight into that. Some of his guests in Cody knew Vance and Rafe from right after the war."

"Outstanding," Duncan said. "That's what he didn't want to tell us."

"You understand why. The three of us, Team Three, have unique contacts with the outside world right now. All of them are fragile. Command needs to let Mac and Shan forge those alliances for the future security of The Vista."

"As far as we've seen, you're the more diplomatic one of the team. You'd do better, being in one of those places." Perro understood his motives had changed, and why. He'd known for months how little control they had over the team.

"We all understand when to talk, when to fight, and when to run."

"You resigned."

"I'm tired of talking, and I don't want to fight. By the end of the year, I'll be set up in central Colorado, and if anyone has an issue, they can come see me personally." His friends, his family, his children, would all be safer with him absent.

"Are you going to be under the jurisdiction of Vance or Caulder?"

"The city is Vance's, for now." Wade meant to sound ominous, but he'd rather negotiate than fight. Fighting had brought humanity to the brink of extinction a generation earlier. They were lucky to be alive. Or something that wasn't luck, but far darker than he cared to consider.

"Will we be able to contact you?"

"After I get established. If I need to contact anyone, I'll do it through one of my team members."

Perro didn't want to understand how they communicated, or how it affected them. "Don't think this means we've abandoned you, or any part of your team. You wanted things to be this way."

"Yes," Wade confirmed.

"One last bit of advice, or an order, if you prefer it to be that way."

"Go ahead."

"Some people may seem to know more about you than you do. Some people may seem to have the best advice you've never heard." Perro knew Wade wasn't gullible, but this was unknown territory for him. "Trust your instinct first."

Wade nodded. "I won't disappoint you."

"Do you know who is reporting back to Council?" Lambert asked Mac, both getting ready to go home, to their parents' houses. It was a little humbling after the past year. The big, bad Security officers, with nowhere to stay while they were in The Vista. A new training class had started and every room in Station Two was occupied. So, home they'd go.

"I think it's a conglomeration, bits of a lot of talk getting back to various people," Mac confessed. "But I could be wrong. If I'd pick one person," he trailed off, not wanting to start more conflict in Security. He'd be back in Cody in a few weeks, so there was no need for added drama.

"Not Taylor?"

"Not anyone. If Council was getting information from outside, there would have been a lot more questions. If someone is talking, it's to Command. Capt. Ballentyne might be one of those special advisors they have for particular situations."

"Advisors, like you were for two years. Like Shan was when she took Green and headed for the coast?"

"Like that, yes."

"Wade never made it a secret. Hell, we partied like madmen when he got that post." Lambert grinned. There would be a party before the team went their separate ways again. 'Conda gatherings could be quite memorable. He'd make sure of it this time.

"Just my opinion," Mac said. "I'll ask him when I see him."

"What are we going to do about our guests from Dakota?"

"We're going to make them our new best friends. We're going to make them feel right at home, just like we have been. When the time comes they decide to go home, and if they invite a diplomatic team from Cody to join them, I'm going to send one. On a volunteer basis, my choice of officers."

"Are you asking me?"

"If you want the job, you'll be in charge of the group."

"Does that come with a promotion?" he asked, peering at his friend as if he cared about a promotion.

"You bet it does," Mac laughed. "If you're not careful, Command will recall Ballentyne and you'll be stuck in charge of Cody by this time next year."

"No, thank you. I don't want the job now or at any point in the foreseeable future. I have plans on retiring to a training position in the next five summers. Find someone with Command aspirations."

"Smart move."

"I hope."

"I want to get to Black Hills before winter sets in."

"You have no idea how shocked I am," Lambert said. "Mick and I can take care of the business end of Cody. Don't piss off Command.

Tell them what you're doing this time. Tell them and let them do all the talking they do so well. Otherwise, I really will be running the place this year."

"You're right," Mac agreed. "On all counts."

"Speaking of that, where did Green get away to?"

"He's out at the Ranchlands. Tribal business. He's been gone for months, with the rest of us."

"Is he going back to Cody?"

"The conversation hasn't come up. We've been here hours, Den. No one is running back to Cody right now. Take a break while you can."

Lambert nodded. "Did you hear what you just said?"

"Sure," Mac said. "I get it."

"Has Wade gone to see his kids?" Lambert had concerns, and that was one of them. It wouldn't be like Wade to not make them a priority.

"Twice this afternoon," Mac said. "With no goading."

"I don't expect him to stay until autumn."

"Neither do I. If he's here a week, I'll be surprised. The thing is, he's on a schedule. You've worked with him long enough to recognize that." Mac picked up his bags and headed downstairs, Lambert right behind him. They had one shot at a ride, because Security was not a taxi service. He doubted he'd uttered those words first, but he'd repeated them many times over his years in Security.

"When he disappears, he's a civilian, and he's on his own?"

"Officially." Mac rubbed his neck, tired. More than tired, but he didn't have an accurate word for it. He wasn't even certain what time it was, other than after midnight.

"You think all the yelling and lecturing and demoting was for show?"

"Not at all. We need to remember our priorities."

"Meaning what?" Lambert asked.

"We couldn't win a war against Estes Park, and more importantly, we don't want a war with them. That's not what we do, it's not why we wanted to get out beyond The Vista. We want to know what they're doing, who their friends are, and who their enemies are, in no particular order."

"Security won't let them walk all over us."

"No, not at all."

"Because what happened in Cody..."

"Will be dealt with appropriately," Mac told him. "If you need to hear about it, you will."

"You don't have to protect us from what you expect to find out there, not anymore."

"That's my job."

"That's our job, to protect The Vista. Stop thinking you need to do this by yourself. I don't mean only you. I mean Team Three."

"Command disbanded the team."

"So what? Are you going to stop being a team now?"

Mac sighed. "You know better than that."

"Start sharing some of that responsibility. We aren't afraid of what you are."

A persistent knock on the side door interrupted Shan before she could get to bed. A hot shower was all she managed, her gear strewn across the bedroom she'd occupied on and off for ten years.

"What is that?" Hunter asked, mostly asleep. He'd insisted on staying in the living room, on the sofa for about ten minutes, until he found out how uncomfortable it was. The cot shoved in a corner of Shan's room was his next choice. She called him old-fashioned before going to shower.

"Someone is kicking down the kitchen door," she told him, pulling on jeans and a tee shirt.

"For real?"

"I don't think so." 9mm in hand, she went to find out. "It's five in the morning," she announced, throwing the door open for Taylor, the one that was her twin.

"It's nice to see you, too," he said, giving her a quick hug. They hadn't had a chance to talk earlier. "Alone?"

"No. What's going on?" She had her radio, always, and it hadn't even bleeped from static. Not an emergency, then.

"Mac, or Hunter?"

"Does it matter?"

A trick question. "I need your opinion, and your attention for, well, another meeting. A secret sort of meeting."

"Now?" she expressed her annoyance.

"Yeah, actually we should. We have to. If Mac is here, we can to talk outside."

"Mac isn't here," Hunter said as he joined them in the kitchen. "If you think you can talk with me, go ahead."

"I need her, for a few minutes."

"Where?" Shan wasn't sure she could drive, or talk.

"Right here is good, if you two are alone," Taylor said. "Is anyone else here?"

"No," she said, curiosity getting the better of her. "Michael is working on the grid at the radio station and Deirdre is on duty for another hour. No other officers."

"Good," he said, leaning out the door and whistling. "I need your opinion."

"You said that."

He shook his head, and held the door open. Lambert came in, carrying a pack, and followed by a tall, raven-haired figure even Shan hadn't expected.

"Kaden," Hunter said before she could.

"Before you ask," Taylor said. "Yes, he's been cleared by Security." He closed the door, leaving it unlocked. It would raise suspicions if it was locked. The Allen house was a way point for Security. Officers used the spare rooms as needed. Knocking first was out of an abundance of caution, and to be polite. Taylor didn't want to know the details of her personal life.

"This isn't my first time in The Vista," Kaden told her. "Even if you think you're aware of everything that happens here, you aren't."

"I figured out that I was wrong sometimes, a few months ago," Shan conceded, still surprised she hadn't known. "Why are you here?"

"You aren't asking the right questions."

"And that's why you're here," Hunter said. There wasn't out-and-out contempt, but he didn't like the outlander.

"That's why I'm here."

"I thought of you earlier today," Shan told Kaden, not adding that it was when Command had been yelling at them.

"Of course you did. A forewarning."

Lambert put his pack on the table and opened it, pulling out a dinner-plated size of scrap metal.

"I've seen this at your house," Taylor said.

"When I shot down that first Black Hawk, five years ago, it was damned near straight overhead. This is part of the debris. It went through the roof of my car and landed in the back seat. I kept it as a souvenir."

"Touch it," Kaden said to her, grinning, making it sound suggestive. He didn't know Taylor was her brother, but he had a good idea about Hunter.

Hunter wanted to punch him.

"No," Shan said. "I don't put on a show for just anyone."

"Look," Lambert got impatient, flipping it over.

Shan did. There was a line of charred paint along one jagged edge. "Nothing any of you can't see."

"Russian?" Hunter asked.

"Yes," Kaden answered. "The Russians bought a number of them, a few years before it all went away."

"You told me in January that you didn't have the ability or the authority to help us," Shan reminded him. "Here you are, telling us things you shouldn't."

"Because you eliminated Rafe and changed the savoir faire of the entire Front Range in one afternoon."

She stared, then shook her head.

"The social and political positions of everyone involved," Kaden confirmed. "Including me and mine."

"I'm aware of what you meant. What questions am I supposed to ask?" Shan gingerly brushed away soot with a fingertip, revealing red paint.

"Caulder has been honest with you, at least. Ask him to tell you what he knows about us, about The Sixth."

"Is she safe there?" Hunter asked.

Kaden regarded him. "Do you mean, would he do her harm, if he found out she's one of The Altered?"

"You know what I mean."

"Your father isn't indiscriminate. He doesn't react without reason. Capt. Allen wouldn't be in danger from him, or the Assembly, unless they had reason to believe she posed a threat to them. I don't mean the simple fact that she's an Altered. They're more progressive than you give them credit for. I assume Vance gave you that fear."

"Lt. Allen," Taylor correct.

"Oh is that so?" Hunter asked, not having heard that yet.

"Ask Caulder what? Vance said Angelfire wouldn't accept an alliance with The Vista, because of us." Shan remembered the conversation well.

"Ask me what corporation created Vance, and what it means to you."

"Fine," she said, too tired to play mind games with him, knowing he'd win even if she was rested. "What corporation created Vance?"

"Skoltech, the Skolkovo Biomedical International conglomerate."

"What does that mean to us?" Lambert asked.

"Skoltech was a massive corporation, headquartered in Moscow. They were among the first to get funding for human genetic manipulation." She'd read about it, sometime years ago, a tiny blurb on a news feed overlooked by the censors. "What corporation created Rafe?" Shan's voice dropped.

"Now you're beginning to see our dilemma. Rafe was created by the SeaTac Metro Technologies Group."

Taylor had the sense not to utter a sound, to not even blink. He'd heard that name before.

"Why does this concern me, or The Vista?" she asked. He'd said to ask the right questions and she had to figure out what those were.

"Rafe and Vance held the Front Range, and they had their own arrangement, for their own reasons. You and your friends did away with Rafe, leaving Vance to his own devices. Which would be good for all of us, except that he's afraid of The Vista, and its potential."

"How does it all tie in?" Taylor was confused.

"Vance was part of the ground war you think happened, somewhere on the continent, sometime twenty years ago. Ask me the right question," Kaden told her. "You haven't put the pieces in the right order. What else was Vance adamant about?"

"He said, stay out of Texas," she remembered. "Who's in Texas?"

"Texans," Lambert offered.

"For the past twenty plus years," Kaden told them, "Texas has been a territory of the Russian Federation."

"Vance is Russian," she stated.

"Not his real name, by the way," Kaden said.

"Are we in danger of an invasion?" Shan asked.

"From them? No. Your concern should be with Vance himself. Consider the source. It's safer for you to think everything he told you is the opposite of the truth. Wade suspected, as soon as they crossed paths. I gave you fair warning. You missed the hints."

"If they came for us, ten years ago, who would have given the order?"

"That is a good question," Kaden pointed out. "In fact, it's a damned good question. You can answer this one."

"Vance," Lambert said.

"And Lambert's nothing close to being an Altered," Kaden smirked at the officer. "Vance came out of Texas, looking for allies, looking for Altered allies. He found Rafe. With the entire continent wide open, they began making plans to divide and conquer. The problem was, some of the others who gathered were Altered, and our kind were trained to be adversaries, to gravitate away from each other. Rafe was a Sixth. That made him different. Vance couldn't break away, no matter what he wanted."

"He tired of having to answer to Rafe, so he set us up to do his dirty work." Shan realized Kaden might be doing the same, but his words felt truthful. It answered the question definitively, for her, of who'd tried to assassinate them.

"Not that difficult, once he realized you'd wandered across Rafe's home turf. All he had to do was sit back and wait for Rafe to act on a perceived aggression. You weren't children anymore."

"So either outcome would work in Vance's favor."

"It would," Kaden agreed.

"We killed the wrong one," Hunter said.

"That being said, you need to know two things," Kaden told them. "First, Rafe would have eventually targeted you if you hadn't gotten to him first. Civilian casualties never concerned him, but active Altered did. The other, there's nothing you can do about Vance. From what we can determine, he's still a Russian operative. Eliminating him would be an act of war."

~ end of Book 2 ~

For More

For more -

The Wildblood Series

Backlash: Prequel to The Wildblood

Trilogy 1

The Vista: Book 1 of The Wildblood
Renegades: Book 2 of The Wildblood
Bloodlines: Book 3 of The Wildblood

novellas

Outliers: Team Two
Outliers: Texas

More to come!

In case you missed it -

Backlash: Prequel to The Wildblood
Introducing Team Three

Facing an unknown adversary that threatens to wreak havoc across what little humanity remains, they must rely on their unusual abilities, and hope they're strong enough to stop the chaos.

The first to join Security, **Mac** is the outsider despite knowing he's as different as his partners. All three are Gen En, genetically enhanced, and he understands it's not a safe thing to be.

Wade is their unofficial leader. Few people outside the team have his trust, making him seem difficult and distant. He's protecting everyone by hiding what they are.

As the Scout, **Shannon** keeps watch on the long-abandoned roadways. This gives her time to consider what might exist beyond Montana. More curious than afraid, she wants to see for herself.

Together, they are unstoppable. Their enemies are gathering.

The Vista: Book 1 of The Wildblood

It's not a dystopia, it's not a utopia - it's their home, and they'd do anything to protect it.

World War Last pushed humanity to the brink of extinction. In the space of ten hours, civilization was gone.
Cut off from the chaos of a pandemic mutated by nuclear war, a group of survivors gathered in a secluded mountain valley. Those that lived through the winter founded The Vista.

But this isn't about the survivors, it's about the first generation after. Twenty years later, children of The Vista have become guardians of their secluded valley. A dark secret, that a few of them are different, something of urban legend, draws them together to protect their home. Venturing out into the world will be more dangerous than anything they've faced.

What they are might save them. It could destroy them. Their enemies know.

Welcome to the world of The Wildblood.

Trust is dangerous; ignorance is deadly.

And next -

Bloodlines: Book 3 of The Wildblood

Learning the truth about the Altered, and the legacy of The Vista, is the first priority of Team Three. It may earn them exile from their home. They know this. **Failure is not an option.**

Loyalty has its price. So does revenge. Someone has to pay.

Also by S. A. Hoag

On another world, in another time, there is -

Tau Scorpii: The Myth of SolTerra

Left to live or die on their own, scattered Terran clans struggle against the elements, other species, and each other. They don't know how or why they're on Sedna, but they are. It's about to get even more difficult to survive. The weather is changing, and no one knows what's next. A group of warriors must make peace with each other while looking for clues to their past. The alternative is extinction.

About the Author

S. A. Hoag is an author, artist, amateur astronomer ("I just look at the stars, I can't tell you their names."), hockey fan, and accidental desert-dweller. Born in the middle of the Rocky Mountains of Colorado, she has lived in a number of cities, in a number of states, and is off on another adventure when not writing or painting. Science Fiction has always been her first interest in reading and writing. Many other genres sneak into the novels and that's all right with her.

www.topaz08.com